A BOX OF BONES

MARINA COHEN

Roaring Brook Press

New York

Text copyright © 2019 by Marina Cohen
Illustrations copyright © 2019 by Yana Bogatch
Published by Roaring Brook Press
Roaring Brook Press is a division of Holtzbrinck Publishing Holdings Limited
Partnership
175 Fifth Avenue, New York, NY 10010
mackids.com

Library of Congress Control Number: 2018955830
ISBN 978-1-250-17221-1

Our books may be purchased in bulk for promotional, educational, or business
use. Please contact your local bookseller or the Macmillan Corporate and
Premium Sales Department at (800) 221-7945 ext. 5442 or by email at
MacmillanSpecialMarkets@macmillan.com.

First edition, 2019
Book design by Cassie Gonzales
Printed in the United States of America by LSC Communications,
Harrisonburg, Virginia

10 9 8 7 6 5 4 3 2 1

For my husband, Michael. Always.

"Sometimes fiction is a way of coping with the poison of the world in a way that lets us survive it."

Neil Gaiman (*The View from the Cheap Seats*)

1

The Man in the Pink Fedora

The man in the pink fedora had no face. He looked like an unfinished wax mannequin dressed in a crisp black tuxedo. He cocked his head and turned slowly toward Kallie.

Even with no eyes, it was as though he were staring right at her. Right into her. He touched the brim of his hat, nodded once, and then vanished into the crowd.

"Did you see that?" Kallie's voice was sharp, her expression dauntless.

Many twelve-year-olds would have been frightened. At the very least, unnerved. Kallie was neither. She had read Darwin. She knew facial expression was an important feature of ancestral social communication, and the very idea that someone dared walk around faceless served only to annoy her.

"See what?" Grandpa Jess tried to follow the jagged path of her gaze, but it lost itself in the labyrinth of people, performers, and sidewalk cafés.

The man was gone. Kallie sighed. "Nothing important. Never mind."

Raven-feather clouds had flocked the sky over Lake Champlain, turning daylight to dusk. The air was thick and unstable. It was sure to storm, but this didn't seem to worry the masses that had come to the marketplace in droves for the annual Festival of Fools.

Kallie wore sturdy rubber boots and a water-resistant jacket over a sensible denim skirt. She carried an umbrella almost as large as those hovering over the outdoor tables like enormous black and green mushroom caps. She subscribed to the Scouts' motto: Be prepared.

"Relax, Kaliope," said Grandpa Jess. "Try to have fun."

"People who relax rarely achieve a thing." She checked her watch and then pressed her thick black frames higher on the bridge of her nose.

Grandpa Jess's mustache twitched. He patted her head. "You can't plan your whole life. And even if you could, you'd miss out on a lot of interesting things."

Though her brown hair was pulled back in a painfully tight ponytail, she smoothed it nonetheless and frowned.

She turned her attention to a woman wearing a shimmering blue leotard standing on her elbows. The woman's legs contorted over her body, steadying a bow and arrow. Her toes released their grip, and the arrow flew, striking a target about twenty feet away. The crowd cheered.

Kallie clutched the handle of her umbrella with one hand and took her grandfather's plaid shirtsleeve with the other. She dragged him farther along the bricked street, walking with purposeful steps. The quicker they moved, the quicker she could leave.

They passed beneath a canopy of lights stretching outward from a giant post that hung suspended, almost like magic, in the intersection of Church and College. It was late afternoon, but darkness had swept the landscape. The delicate bulbs twinkled like tiny jars filled with fireflies.

All around her the air was steeped in powerful aromas: piping hot coffee from Speeder &
Earl's; Ken's gooey cheese pizza; caramel apples
from Lake Champlain Chocolates; sweet and salty
kettle corn; and paper-thin crêpes filled with
strawberries and cream from the Skinny Pancake
cart.

Kallie's olfactory system clicked to overload. She
wrinkled her nose as she wove through the throng,
past a man on a ten-foot unicycle, a belly dancer, and
a juggler in a plum patchy vest tossing flaming sticks
high into the air.

Over the din, a haunting melody crackled from a
loudspeaker. Outside Vermont Violins, a sad-faced
clown in a red velvet suit eased a bow across delicate
strings.

"How about a treat?" asked Grandpa Jess, stopping at the end of a lineup winding toward an ice-
cream shop. In the narrow space between his beard
and brows, his eyes crinkled with delight.

"Ice cream is fourteen percent cholesterol. Not to
mention thirty-five percent fat."

"Haven't you heard?" said Grandpa Jess. "Fat is

now the sixth food group." He pinched her upper arm with a meaty hand. "Or is it the seventh?"

"Good fat, Grandpa. Like nuts. And beans."

"Perfect. We'll have Rocky Road. It has almonds. And chocolate is made from a bean."

She rolled her eyes, then smiled and joined the line.

As they waited, Kallie couldn't help but wonder why so many people were drawn to the festival. Even the mayor himself had kicked off the annual event filled with what he called *awe-inspiring hijinks and rollicking tomfoolery.*

Kallie was no fan of jinks—high or low—or any sort of foolery, be it Tom, Tim, or Harry, but her grandfather had insisted they go. She didn't envy him having to answer to her father for it.

They stood for some time, only inching forward. All the while, the dark clouds grew thicker and tighter. The wind picked up, and Kallie was certain she heard a low murmur of distant thunder.

Nearby, a man in an emerald suit shifted shells around on a small table. When he stopped, a woman guessed which of the three concealed a pea. She smiled self-assuredly at the crowd. Then the man held up her watch for all to see. While she was busy eyeing the shells, he had stolen it right off her wrist.

"Like magic!" the woman gasped.

"Magic," scoffed Kallie. More like distraction and deception. Mind tricks. Didn't these people know there was no such thing as real magic?

Grandpa Jess had moved farther up the line. Kallie was about to catch up when she caught sight of the faceless man. He was smaller and thinner than she'd first imagined. Except for the tuxedo, she wasn't entirely certain it was a man.

He clapped his hands, plucked a fistful of roses from thin air, and began handing them to those gathered nearby. When he arrived in front of Kallie, the roses were gone.

Up close she could see flesh-colored material covered his head, masking his features. Even his hands were concealed. He took off his fedora, flipped it over, and tapped it lightly. Out tumbled a tiny box, which he placed in the palm of her hand.

It was cube-shaped with a variety of ivory-colored circular inlays on each face. There were circles inside circles with elaborate dark designs. The box had no hinges and no clasp. No apparent way of opening it.

Kallie's father had taught her never to accept gifts from strangers. She'd taken the box on reflex, without thinking. She extended her arm to return it, but when she looked up, he was gone again.

A blue flash split the sky above the lake, followed instantly by a loud clap of thunder. Kallie shoved the box into her jacket pocket and snapped open her umbrella just in time. The rain came fast and furious. Enormous drops of water beat so hard against the ground they appeared to bounce back up.

The streets were a blur of motion as everyone scurried for shelter—everyone except a thin girl wearing a bright yellow shirt and matching shorts. She stood with her chin tilted upward; her arms stretched wide to catch the downpour. The rain-soaked shorts clung to her thighs, and her T-shirt was quickly becoming embarrassingly transparent, but she didn't seem to mind. For a moment, her eyes met Kallie's, and the girl's gaunt face lit up with a smile.

A tiny door in Kallie's cobwebbed memory clicked open and something soft and gentle fluttered out. She chased it back inside, sealed the door, and hunkered deep beneath her umbrella. Her father would be upset if she got soaked and caught a cold.

Grandpa Jess waved at Kallie from beneath the awning of the ice-cream shop. When she approached, he disentangled himself from the bodies, bunched like asparagus, and joined her beneath the umbrella.

"Can we please leave, Grandpa?"

He glanced at the sky and nodded sadly. Placing his arm around her shoulder, he took the umbrella handle. They clung together as they made their way along Church Street toward Main. Just before they turned the corner, Kallie took one last look back.

The unicyclist was gone. So was the belly dancer. The juggler's fire sticks had been extinguished, and the pounding rain drowned out the haunting melody of the sad clown's violin.

Everything was gray, as though the rain had washed all color from the world. The girl in yellow twirled and sloshed through the deep puddles, as if dancing to music only she could hear.

Kallie formed a final, fleeting picture in her mind's eye, but there was no sign of the faceless man.

2

A Peculiar Puzzle

"Where were you?"

Kallie's father stood in the narrow doorway. He was tall and lean and wore a perfectly pressed pinstripe suit, accentuating his height. His hair, slick against his skull, was like black glass.

In contrast, Grandpa Jess was a burly, bearded barrel. He wore nothing but faded flannel and well-worn denim. His hair was like a dandelion gone to seed. Kallie worried a good, strong wind might one day blow it right off his head.

She raised an eyebrow at Grandpa Jess in an *I told you so* expression. She closed the umbrella, shook it twice, and then climbed the porch steps to their green-shuttered foursquare in the heart of town.

The neighborhood was known as the Five Sisters because its primary streets were Caroline, Catherine, Charlotte, Margaret, and Marian. Legend had it the streets were named after the five daughters of the original developer, though no one—not even local historians—could confirm or deny the claim. This didn't matter to Kallie, for legends were stories, and stories were lies.

Grandpa Jess had bought the house decades ago, immediately after he married Grandma Geneviève, whom he called Gem. He never moved, not even after she died. Kallie's father returned to the house with Kallie when she was very young. It was right after The Writer had drowned.

Grandpa Jess cleared his throat. "You're early."

"And you're one hour, seven minutes, and thirty-two seconds late." Her father held the screen door open, his eyes steely behind his dark-rimmed glasses.

"We were at the festival," said Kallie, adjusting her matching eye gear.

"For a short time . . ." added Grandpa. He offered a sheepish grin.

Kallie shook the last drips and drops from her umbrella and leaned it against the dull white siding. It was no longer raining, but the air was still a heavy slate-gray.

"The festival? Of *Fools*?" Kallie's father stepped aside and let them pass. The screen door slammed behind. He gave Kallie a peck on the cheek, then eyed Grandpa. "Waste of time and money."

Victor Jones was in charge of risk management at Lake Champlain Insurance, which meant he was responsible for calculating calamity. What were the exact chances a person would be struck by lightning or lose a limb to a rogue shark? What were the precise odds a library would implode? How likely would it be that a meteor would plummet from the sky and land directly on top of the local laundromat?

Most people disliked contemplating dreadful things, so they underestimated the likelihood of such things happening. Luckily, Victor Jones was on the job. He knew tragedy could strike at any moment, and just like Kallie, his motto was: Be prepared.

Kallie removed her boots. She arranged them in perfect order on the mat so they would not leak onto the old pine floor. "I warned him you'd be mad. He didn't listen."

Victor Jones sighed. "Does he ever?" He picked up the shoes Grandpa Jess had flung haphazardly and lined them up as well. "And I wasn't mad. Just worried."

"The festival was fun," said Grandpa, shaking his hair, spraying droplets of rain. "You do remember what fun is, don't you, Victor?"

Kallie's father scowled. He wiped the drips from his cheeks and jacket sleeves. "There's enough nonsense in the world. Kallie doesn't need you exposing her to even more."

"Don't worry, Dad," said Kallie, making a face as though she'd just bitten into a mealy apple. "I didn't enjoy it."

She took off her rain jacket, but as she hung it on the newel post to dry, something knocked against the wood. She reached into the pocket and pulled out the box. She'd forgotten all about it.

"What's that?" asked her father.

"A box."

Kallie tilted it. Something shifted inside.

"I can see it's a box, silly," he said. "Where'd you get it?"

"A man gave it to me. At the festival."

Victor Jones's eyes narrowed. He folded his arms, staring hard at Grandpa. "What man?"

Grandpa Jess shrugged.

"The man in the pink fedora," said Kallie. "He had no face."

"What do you mean he had no face?" Her father's expression contorted, nearly twisting into itself. He suddenly reminded Kallie of the woman in the shimmering blue leotard.

"He was *faceless*. Without face." She examined the surfaces covered in ivory-colored circles and dark etchings. It seemed old. Very old.

"Must have been part of his act," said Grandpa Jess, leaning in for a better look. "There were all sorts of buskers. Magicians, belly dancers, clowns . . ."

"And why would this faceless clown give Kallie a box?" asked her father, his tone a calculated balance between suspicion and anger.

"Because he ran out of roses," she said, sliding her fingernails into the grooves, trying to pry it open.

"Roses?" Her father seemed genuinely confused.

"Yes. He made them appear out of thin air and then—"

Victor Jones waved a dismissive hand. "I thought I taught you never to accept gifts from strangers." He snatched the box from her and held it up to the light. It rattled softly. "Who knows what's inside? Could be dangerous."

"Don't bother," she said. "It doesn't open."

"Let me see that," said Grandpa, taking the cube. He turned it over in his hands, studying it carefully. Kallie watched his bushy eyebrows stitch tightly together and then burst apart as his eyes grew wide. "Why . . . this is a trick box."

"A what?" Kallie and her father said at the same time.

"A secret box. A puzzle box. I've heard of them," he said, running his thick finger over the deep grooves, the corners, and the edges. "Never come across one, though."

"How do you open it?"

"Well, now. That's the trick part." He touched the

tip of her nose. "Some will open with a simple squeeze in the right location." He pressed several spots, but nothing happened. "Others require a sequence of complicated—often obscure—manipulations. Anywhere from two to two thousand moves."

She eyed the box with carefully measured curiosity. She didn't like picture puzzles—they were like artwork cut into pieces, a waste of valuable time. But this was different. "How do you think it works?"

"I'm not sure," said Grandpa. "They're all unique. The man gave it to you—so I guess it's up to you to figure it out." He plopped it back into her hands and winked.

"I'd get rid of that silly thing," said her father. "It'll distract you. You have only a few weeks before school starts. You need to prepare."

Every morning, Victor Jones prepared for work by walking five miles. Running disorganized the brain, he explained to Kallie, but walking helped the mind focus. He liked to be focused.

"It's hardly silly," said Grandpa. "It's quite clever. Mechanical. Let her keep it."

"What's that white material?" Kallie's father pointed to the circles. "Ivory? Maybe the clown kept his face hidden because he's an ivory poacher."

"It's not ivory," said Grandpa. "Ivory is as smooth as butter. This is rutted and pockmarked. Could be shell. Possibly bone. Probably plastic. Tough to tell these days."

Kallie inspected the circles. The shapes, lines, swirls, and curls etched into them seemed random. Her father had taught her about chaos theory. According to it, nothing in life was random. There was an underlying order in even apparently random data— you just had to find the pattern.

"You know, I once heard a story about a box like this . . ." began Grandpa Jess.

Kallie frowned. She turned on her heels and marched upstairs. Over her shoulder she heard her father call, "Toss it out, Kallie. It will only cause trouble."

Kallie's bedroom was tidy and perfectly organized, with minimal distractions. There was a bed, a nightstand, a dresser, and a desk. Beside the desk was a bookshelf with atlases, almanacs, dictionaries, a set of used encyclopedias, a microscope she got for her tenth birthday, and a single faded photograph in a plain brass frame.

On her desk sat her laptop and a neat stack of textbooks. *Culture and Customs of Ancient Civilizations*, *The Joys of Trigonometry*, and *Everything You Need to Know About Quantum Physics, but Were Afraid to Ask*—her light summer reading. On the wall above her desk hung a poster of the periodic table; on the opposite wall, an enormous world map; and over her bed, a giant graphic image of the night sky divided into eighty-eight constellations.

Kallie sat on the edge of her bed so as not to muss the wrinkle-free covers. If the box was mechanical, that meant it was mathematical. She would solve the puzzle just as she solved really tough equations—with patience, hard work, and determination.

She toiled for over an hour, pressing, pushing, and prying, but by dinnertime, she was ready for a break. She set the box on her desk and headed for the kitchen.

Kallie set the table as usual, folded napkins crisply, placed them strategically beside each plate, and aligned cutlery neatly on top.

"*To enjoy good health, to bring true happiness to one's family, to bring peace to all, one must first discipline and control one's own mind,*" she quoted from Buddha.

That night, the storm started up again. Kallie lay in bed teetering on the brink of sleep. She listened to the soothing clatter of rain against her window.

Perhaps it was just the rain, but somewhere, just beneath the gentle *tap, tap, tap,* she could swear she heard another sound. A low rattle—as though something were trapped inside the box, and it was struggling to get out.

3

POSSIBILITIES

The dark waters of the lake had begun to cool, and the nights stretched, eating away at daylight hours with a ravenous appetite.

The final weeks of summer vacation had evaporated like morning mist. Kallie had spent most of her time preparing for school—and trying to solve the mechanism of the puzzle box. She'd pressed, pulled, shifted, lifted, twisted, and pried, all to no avail.

It was late Monday night when she finally accepted her father had been right all along. She had wasted enough time and energy on the box and refused to give it another moment's thought. She would get rid of it first thing in the morning.

Kallie awoke at precisely 6:57 a.m. She always set

an alarm—even on weekends—a whole three minutes ahead of her schedule on the odd chance the clock ran out of sync with standard time while she slept. She reached for her glasses on her nightstand, sat up, and stretched.

She'd nearly forgotten her resolve to get rid of the box until she saw it perched on her desk. She slipped out of bed, picked it up, and prepared to pitch it into her wastepaper basket, when suddenly it shifted, coming alive in her hands.

Kallie dropped the box as though it had bitten her. It thumped against the old pine floor and tumbled to a stop. For a moment, she stood staring at it. In the back of her mind, she could hear her father's voice puncture out the words: *Boxes can't bite*.

She must have applied pressure to the right spot, triggering a move.

Reaching for the box, she held it tightly. It was cold and hard and perfectly immobile. She turned it over and examined the myriad circles inside circles on each of the faces. How had she done it?

Kallie placed the box on her desk beside the textbooks, careful to arrange it in the exact spot, at the exact angle it had been. She paused, replaying the scene in her mind. Once she was ready, her thumb and index finger formed pincers, just as they'd done the first time. She touched two sides, squeezed, and lifted.

Nothing happened.

Kallie set the box back down and flexed her fingers. She lifted it a second time. Still, nothing.

She tried again and again, each time adjusting her hand a smidge this way, a pinch that. She even slid her fingers along the etchings, but nothing moved.

Her gaze swung from the box to the textbooks, and she sighed. The cube had wasted enough precious time. She lifted it one last time to plunk it into the wastebasket when she felt a soft *click*. One of the tiny circles had turned.

The circles. Of course. Kallie kicked herself for not having thought of it sooner. What was the fundamental property of a circle? It turned.

Kallie tried to turn the same circle again, but it was locked in place. She tried reversing the direction, but that didn't work, either. Kallie frowned hard. Then she had an idea.

She turned her attention to all the other circles on that face. She tried each one individually, but none would budge. She turned the cube over and systematically tried all the circles on all the other faces until, at last, one moved a hairsbreadth clockwise.

That was it. You could move only one circle at a time, and then you had to find the next move and the next. Kallie decided the circles worked like the dial in a combination lock. This was the trick Grandpa Jess was talking about. She'd solved the mystery of the mechanism.

There were fifty-seven circles in total. Kallie did some quick calculations. If there were sixty clicks in a full rotation, that meant over three thousand possible moves.

Perhaps, she thought, some circles didn't require a full rotation. Then again, what if others moved beyond a single rotation, maybe two or three full turns? The possibilities could be endless. The designer of the box certainly intended for maximum frustration. A broad grin spread across Kallie's face.

That morning, she made her usual breakfast—a steaming bowl of instant oatmeal with a half teaspoon of brown sugar, two shakes of cinnamon, and ten raisins. After she ate, she returned to her bedroom, explaining to Grandpa Jess she was quite busy and could not be disturbed.

She sat rigidly at her desk. Beside her, she placed a pencil and a notepad in which she would record each move.

Each of the faces had a different number of circles forming a different pattern. She labeled each face from one to six and then labeled each circle according to its size. Once the chart in her notepad was complete, she took a deep breath, and then, slowly, methodically, she began.

After three hours, Kallie had recorded 437 moves. It was tedious work—though not difficult. She knew she was still a long way from opening the box—if, in fact, it did open—but something strange had begun to happen.

The apparently random etchings—the swirls and lines—began to connect, and Kallie understood what it meant. The chaos theory was right—these etchings were not random. Kallie picked up her pace.

She worked for another solid hour before

breaking for lunch. She was getting closer and was now more determined than ever. By late afternoon, she had recorded over two thousand moves, and judging by the way the etchings were connecting, she knew some of the circles had found their final resting place.

There was a sharp knock at the door. Kallie's father poked his head inside. She hadn't heard him come home from the office.

"You haven't set the table yet."

Kallie smiled—a little too widely. "Coming."

He narrowed his eyes and stepped into the room. "What have you been up to?" He looked at her desk and frowned. "Tell me you haven't spent all day on that ridiculous box."

"Grandpa was right," said Kallie. She held up her notepad, now filled with pages and pages of moves. "It's mechanical."

He sighed. "I suppose determination is a virtue." He was about to leave but then paused. He added, a little softer than Kallie was used to, "Just don't expect anything from it. I'd hate to see you disappointed. It's only a box."

She nodded and stood. They left the room together and entered the kitchen. To mark the end of summer vacation, Grandpa Jess made a special meal consisting of *tourtière*—a flaky crust filled with minced pork and potatoes—maple baked beans, and garlic toast. They were Grandma Gem's recipes, handed down to her from her *mémé*.

Once Kallie had finished eating, she cleared the dishes and returned immediately to her room. She had recorded nearly three thousand moves, but it was getting late. Soon it would be bedtime. She had to work quickly.

Most of the faces were complete. Kallie could see the patterns clearly. On one of the faces were two stars. On another, two stars and a full circle. On a third, two stars and a half circle. The fourth, two stars and a crescent.

Like the phases of the moon, thought Kallie.

Though exhausted, she continued at a feverish pace. Her fingers moved independently of her mind. One more move. Just one more. Another. And another. And at last, it was done. All the circles had reached their final resting place.

She lifted the box to have a closer look when suddenly the full circle at the bottom of the box flipped open and something scattered across the floor. The large cube had given birth to smaller cubes.

Kallie dropped to her knees. She set the box beside her and gathered the pieces into a line. There were nine in total, all made from the same ivory-colored substance as the circle inlay.

Each of the tiny cubes had etchings forming pictures. She made a mental note of the images facing upward. Then she picked up one of the pieces. There were different images on each of its six faces.

What could this be? Kallie wondered. Some sort of game? She had a game of Yahtzee tucked away in her closet. Grandpa had given it to her two years ago for her tenth birthday. It had five dice. You had to toss them and try for specific combinations.

Kallie gathered the pieces, cupping them in both hands.

"Bedtime!" her father boomed from the hall.

Kallie never had to be reminded. His voice startled her, and her hands came apart, scattering the pieces a second time. As one by one she lined them up, her stomach clenched and her eyes grew wide. They had landed on the exact same pictures.

As best as she could tell, the first was some kind of animal with sharp ears and a pointed snout. The second was a goblet with a jagged line down the center. Beside it, an egglike shape with holes. Then a castle; a cylinder spouting flames; a coffin; a skull; and a long pointed object, like a knife or a dagger. The final piece had no carvings at all. It was blank.

Kallie knew the probability of the five-dice game well. She and her friend Pole had once figured it out— just for fun. Five dice, each with six sides, meant 7,776 possible combinations. How many possibilities could there be for nine pieces? Eight if you excluded the blank.

Kallie calculated. It was in the millions. Millions of possibilities, and the pieces had landed on the same pictures, in the same order, a second time. There was a greater chance Kallie would be struck by lightning.

Slowly, carefully, she picked up the cubes. She had to try again. No way could they land on the same pictures a third time. Her hands trembled as she shook them and let them fall.

"Lights out," her father called. "Tomorrow's the first day of school. You need your rest."

Kallie tried to respond, but her throat had gone as dry as desert dust. She opened her mouth, but no sound escaped.

The pictures. They were all the same.

With trembling hands, Kallie stuffed the pieces back into the open circle. In the instant she sealed it, every circle on every face began to spin backward, like clockwork, and a soft melody began to play. It was a low, mournful tune that burrowed deep into Kallie's brain like a breeding sand flea.

Then, all at once, the spinning and the music stopped.

Kallie seized the box, tore open her closet, and flung the thing into the farthest corner, slamming the door shut. But it was too late. Something had changed. The room felt colder. And darker. And a high-pitched howl echoed from somewhere outside.

Kallie crept to her window and peeled back the curtain. In the middle of the deserted street stood an animal. It appeared to be a cross between a fox and a wolf. It glared up at Kallie with amethyst eyes, its pearly coat shimmering in the moonlight.

Something else had escaped the box. Something other than the pieces. Something that could not be stuffed back inside.

4

THE JACKAL

Evil had spread throughout the land. It seeped into the earth of the fields, infecting all that grew. It lingered in the dying branches of old trees. Its black breath bent every blossom, every blade of grass, and every weed from the Sallow River to the Burning Mountains, from the ancient forests to the poor villages. All that had once flourished under the benevolent Empress now soured under the reign of her only child.

In the darkest hours of the early morn, the old bone carver and his apprentice left the mud-brick walls and thatched roof of their meager workshop and set out upon a long and desolate road.

It was the eve of Barterfest—the one time each year merchants were permitted into the palace to sell their goods.

The bone carver was a poor man with no cart or oxen. It was a long journey to the palace on foot, and so he prepared for an early start.

"Is it true, Master?" asked Liah. "Does she bathe in a blood pond?"

The bone carver did not respond. Instead, he pulled the drawstring tighter on his hemp-fiber sack and slung it over his shoulder. In it, he carried many precious carvings, wrapped in silk for added protection.

Liah was lucky to have such a wise and honorable master. He was a skilled carver—the best in the land. He knew how to prepare bones—how to wash and bleach them, how to perform the ancient rituals that released the spirit from its mortal bind.

In the nights before the journey, he had made many sacrifices to his dead ancestors. If they were pleased, the child Empress would find favor in his workmanship and pay him richly. If they were displeased, she would reject his wares and he would leave the palace empty-handed.

Liah was a foundling. There were no bones for her to honor. No sacrifices to be made. And no ancestors to determine her fate.

The sack of provisions she carried drew her shoulders

straight. In it were several hard millet cakes and two large gourds filled with water that had been boiled and cooled. To the sack she had secretly added two of her own carvings—a musical instrument and a thin dagger—to see if perhaps she might be allowed to present them to the Empress.

"I have heard she keeps a forest of meat where she feasts on the flesh of her enemies," said Liah.

The bone carver stopped. He wagged a calloused finger. "The parrot is a foolish bird, for it repeats what it hears with little knowledge and less thought." He paused, peered side to side, and then added softly, "The Empress has many spies. Speaking evil of her invites bad fortune."

Liah had heard many tales about the child Empress. Some villagers said she could turn water to stone. Others claimed she could melt the stars in the sky and make it rain gold. Some said she was a great and powerful sorceress who could charm snakes and scorpions with but a single word. Liah had even heard she could shift form and roamed the land in disguise, observing her enemies unseen.

There were so many whisperings it was difficult to sift granules of truth from bushels of lies. Yet all were in agreement: Though young, the Empress was dangerously cruel, slaughtering mercilessly all who opposed her. Liah might have been worried were she not under the protection of the wise and venerable bone carver.

The two continued for some time in darkness past the empty marketplace, the last of the village homes, and through the grassy fields toward the river's edge. Another few steps and it would be as far as Liah had ever been allowed to venture.

When at last the cinnamon sun bled over the horizon, their path entered a dense wood where gnarled trees huddled like frightened giants, their roots interwoven in lacy patterns over the parched earth. What little light managed to pierce the thick canopy only served to deepen the shadows. The air was cool and smacked of decay. Liah pulled her brown cloak tighter around her shoulders.

They had traveled a great distance, and Liah's feet had begun to blister. She stopped to rub her heel. The bone carver wore goatskin shoes, which protected his feet. Liah's were made of straw woven together with flax thread. They were rough and thinning.

"When might we rest?" she huffed.

The bone carver glanced about nervously. "This is an ancient forest, haunted by the spirits of those who perished without ancestors to provide their bones with a proper burial. *Remain on the path. And do not disturb anything. We will rest once we reach the crossroads.*"

Liah pressed onward, but after several more hours, she grew weary and began to lag. Each time she skipped to catch up, the burst of energy cost her dearly, and she slipped farther behind.

As she walked, she kept a sharp eye on the shadowy maze. Gray rocks. Brown crusted leaves. Blackish-green moss. Then, all at once, she stopped and squinted, for something had caught her eye.

Not far off the path lay the remains of a small creature—perhaps a badger or a young hare. It was a lucky find. The bone carver rarely gave Liah her own pieces to carve, and when he did, they were tiny fragments, hardly useful. If a large piece was intact, Liah might boil it, bleach it in sunlight, and carve from it a crescent-shaped comb or a butterfly hairpin.

She had been warned to stay on the path and to touch nothing. But the bones were too precious to resist. Liah took a tentative step toward them, then another, and another, until she stood within reach. All around her grew silent and still.

The carcass at her feet had been stripped clean by

scavenger birds and insects. Clumps of matted fur lay strewn about, but there was no stench of death; the creature had perished some time ago. Liah reached for the longest and strongest piece—a hind leg bone—and as her hand gripped its hard, rutted surface, the surrounding silence was broken by the soft snap of a twig.

Her body tensed as her eyes darted in the direction of the sound. She sensed movement but could see none. She was about to turn when something emerged from the lacy shadows.

Liah had never seen anything quite like it before. They stood studying each other, but when Liah took a small step backward, the creature's hind legs crouched, preparing to spring.

In her satchel was the small dagger—one of her precious carvings—but there was no time to retrieve it. Instead, her grip tightened on the bone in her hand, and as the beast leaped toward her, she flung it as hard as she could, narrowly missing her target.

Her hands flew to her face, and the curtains of her eyes drew shut. She let out a strangled yelp, awaiting the sharp sting of barbed teeth.

5

SOMETHING YELLOW THIS WAY COMES

Blip, blip, blip . . . Blip, blip, blip . . .

The alarm pinged softly. Kallie opened her eyes. She took a deep breath, exhaled, and smiled. It was the last Wednesday in August—the first day of school in the state of Vermont.

The new day brought with it new perspective. Kallie decided there were simple, logical explanations for all the strange happenings of the previous night.

First, dice could be loaded—weighted down from the inside so they would always land on the same number. It was an old trick used by crooked gamblers.

Second, just as Grandpa Jess had said, the box was mechanical. By turning the circles, Kallie must have cranked the mechanism, and then, like a wind-up toy, it was set to play music as it unwound.

And last, she had been overtired. Exhaustion could cause hallucinations. Frighteningly real hallucinations. The animal she'd seen the previous night was no wolf—it was probably nothing more than a stray dog. She scolded herself for having allowed emotions to trick her senses and rattle her security.

Kallie slipped out of bed and stretched. She had selected an entire week's wardrobe a month in advance. All she needed to do was reach for the hanger in her closet labeled *Wednesday*. She opened the door and was greeted with undulating waves of navy, gray, white, and black.

The first day of school was important. It would set the tone for the year, so she'd chosen a white button-down shirt and a gray jumper. She liked that it resembled a uniform even though her school required none.

She snatched the hanger and shut the door, not even glancing at the box that lay hidden in shadow. Luckily, the long-range forecast said it would be warm and sunny all week—no jacket or umbrella would be necessary.

She ate her usual breakfast, packed a nutritious lunch, and prepared her bag, equipping it with plenty of sharpened pencils, several erasers, two boxes of tissues, and five bottles of hand sanitizer. Most kids carried backpacks, but Kallie preferred a leather satchel. It had a variety of compartments for maximum organization.

"All set?" said Grandpa, reaching for his Catamounts cap.

Kallie slung her bag over her shoulder, stepped into her black Oxford shoes, and proceeded down the porch steps.

The school was exactly 1.2 miles from her house—2,543 steps according to her watch, which doubled as a fitness tracker. They weren't even halfway there when she began to slow.

"What's wrong?" asked Grandpa Jess. "Case of the first-day jitters?"

Kallie frowned. "Certainly not. You know I love school." She stooped to rub her ankles. "I'm just tired,

I guess." She had missed her regular bedtime, had tossed and turned most of the night, and now she was paying for it.

Out of the corner of her eye, she glimpsed a streak of white. Her head snapped in its direction, but nothing was there. She took a deep breath, gathered herself, and then trundled the rest of the way to the old three-story brick school.

"I can take it from here," she said.

Grandpa Jess gave her a tight squeeze. Kallie watched him cross the street and disappear toward the lake. He never missed an opportunity to take his boat out on the lake.

There were a few minutes before the first entry bell, so Kallie stood off to one side listening to kids buzz excitedly about summer adventures and lament the loss of freedom. She was happy to be back at school. She much preferred strict routine and rigid schedules to the paralyzing pandemonium known as *free time*.

"Hey," said Pole. "How was summer?"

"Perfectly predictable." Kallie grinned. "Yours?"

"Unequivocally uneventful."

It was their usual post–summer vacation greeting. They both chuckled.

Though Kallie was not disliked by anyone in particular, she had very few of what she considered friends. Her best friend, if you could call him that, was Napoleon Rodriguez.

Pole understood Kallie. Like her, he lacked coordination, excelled in math and science, and had no time for frivolities known as *the arts*.

He had two older brothers who were away studying chemical engineering in New Hampshire, so, like Kallie, he, too, was the only child in a house of adults. And, just like her, he disliked his full name, Napoleon. Unfortunately, with his short stature, deep-set eyes, and brown hair, he bore a striking resemblance to the French dictator.

Kaliope Jones had been named after the muse of epic poetry and eloquence. In Greek, her name meant *lovely voice*. A great joke *The Writer* had played on her, since Kallie despised poetry, and when she opened her mouth to sing, the music teacher, Mr. Pagliacci, would often say, "Just mouth the words, dear, or you'll ruin it for the rest of the children." She'd tried to change her name to Pythagoras in third grade. Sadly, it didn't stick.

"Do anything interesting?" asked Pole.

"As a matter of fact," said Kallie, "I spent the entire month of July relating the Fibonacci sequence to nature. It's extremely prevalent in the petals of various daisies . . . and don't even get me started on pine cones."

"Interesting," said Pole. "I spent my summer on pi. I've memorized 356 digits. Did you know that if you measured the meandering distance of a river from its source to its mouth, and compared that with its direct distance, it's approximately pi? You can find pi in light and sound, in a supernova, and in apples. In fact, pi can show up in the strangest of places . . ."

"Did someone say apple pie? I adore apple pie!" trilled an excited voice. "Though my favorite is strawberry-rhubarb—especially during the month of June when strawberries are in season and so much sweeter than when they have to bring them all the way up north from Florida or California or Mexico. Spending all that time in refrigeration drains the sweetness, don't you think?"

The girl gave them no chance to reply before her mouth was moving again.

"Of course, I love other pies—like key lime and peach—with a crumble top, not that lacy kind which is just extra crust that, if you ask me, belongs on the bottom. I tried mincemeat once, and, do you know, it's not meat at all—"

"Ahem." Pole cleared his throat, interrupting her soliloquy. "Who exactly are you?"

Kallie stood staring, stony-faced. The girl was no longer soaking wet, and as a result her hair seemed significantly lighter—and shorter—but Kallie recognized her all the same. It was the rain-dancing girl in yellow.

"I'm *Velikaya Knyazhna Anastasiya Nikolayevna Romanova*—named after my great-great-grandmother, the Grand Duchess, daughter of Tsar Nikolai the second, last sovereign of Russia. And you are?"

Kallie examined the girl, as thin and short as Pole, with huge teeth and a smile that took up her entire face. She was wearing the same yellow T-shirt now over a pair of faded jeans two inches too short. Her purple backpack was soiled, and the seams were frayed. It was stuffed to splitting. She did not look at all like the great-great-granddaughter of a Grand Duchess.

"I'm Pole," he said, extending a rigid hand.

The girl grasped it in both of hers and rung it like a bell. "Pleased to meet you, Paul."

Kallie's hands remained stiffly at her sides. "Pole. Not Paul."

Pole smiled. "She's Kallie."

The girl studied Kallie, a hint of recognition lighting up her eyes. She tilted her head, put a finger to her lips, and then pointed, tapping the air between them. "I know you from somewhere. I'm good with faces. Have we met before? Perhaps in a past life?"

The crease between Kallie's eyes deepened, and her lips drew thin. "You get only one life," she said through gritted teeth.

"Oh, I've had hundreds," said the girl, chuckling and shaking her head. "I've been an Egyptian princess, a coal miner, some kind of protozoan . . ." She seemed to linger on this thought for a moment before proceeding. "A snow leopard, a yellow-bellied swallow . . . Oh, I really liked that life . . ." She closed her eyes and took a deep breath. "Sometimes, I still feel like I can fly . . ."

The bell rang. Kallie heaved a sigh of relief. The girl's chatter was exhausting. It was making her dizzy.

"Well, we'd best get inside before you take wing." She turned sharply and made her way toward the steps. "Saved by the bell," she muttered.

"Yeah," said Pole. "Right." Though Kallie noticed he kept glancing over his shoulder.

Kallie clutched her satchel and paced steadily into the flow of traffic, leaving the new girl behind in the frothy current of excited bodies. She and Pole were in Mr. Bent's sixth-grade homeroom this year, and Kallie couldn't be happier. Since they didn't have locker assignments yet, she went straight to her class, satchel in tow.

Mr. Bent stood in the doorway. He wore a crisp blue shirt and a black bow tie under a white lab coat. He had the reputation of being the best science teacher in the school. The entire country, if you asked him.

"Welcome," he said. "Hello. Step right on in and take your seat . . ."

Desks had been arranged in neat rows with

names printed on white cards placed on top of each. The walls were free from cheerful clutter, the bulletin boards trimmed in plain black borders, and the shelves perfectly organized. Kallie took a deep breath. She already felt at home.

Nearly all the desks were filled with the usual suspects by the time the second bell sounded. The voice of Principal McEwan crackled over the intercom with his customary first-day speech sounding like he was talking to them from Mars. Once announcements were over, Mr. Bent took over.

"Welcome to sixth grade," he said. "This year will prove to be quite rigorous, with plenty of homework and absolutely no wasted time."

There came a chorus of groans, while Kallie nodded approvingly.

"Shortly, I will be assigning lockers, but first I will take attendance. Pole, can you pass out the timetables?"

Mr. Bent had a brusque, no-nonsense voice. He called each name sharply, and each was met with a *Here* or *Present*. When Billy Whibbs tried to say *Yo*, Mr. Bent paused, looked over his pince-nez glasses, and waited patiently until Billy cleared his throat and in a far less enthusiastic voice whispered, *Present*.

Mr. Bent was halfway through the roll call when the door burst open. He stopped, and everyone stared as the girl in yellow with the huge purple backpack tumbled inside.

"Sorry I'm late. I've never been in a school. I got lost in the labyrinth of twisting hallways and stairwells and . . ."

"Yes, well," said Mr. Bent. "Take your seat, Miss . . ."

"Anastasiya Romanova," she announced proudly.

The teacher frowned. He searched his attendance list. "There doesn't appear to be an *Anastasiya Romanova* on my list." He adjusted his pince-nez and looked at her squarely. "There is, however, an Anna Glud."

"Of course. Yes. It would say that," said the girl. "After all, my great-great-grandmother had to escape execution. Bolshevik revolutionaries have been trying to track us down for over a century. Officially, I go by my father's surname. Purely for safety purposes."

"I see," said the teacher dully. "Well, aside from

the fact that any rumors of the survival of Anastasiya Romanov have long since been conclusively and scientifically disproven via DNA analysis, and due to the necessity of the school to use your *official* name, I will be referring to you as Anna Glud. Now, please take your seat, Miss Glud."

Anna nodded cheerfully, and then her smile broadened when she found her name tag on a desk right beside Kallie. She kept trying to catch her eye, but Kallie kept her gaze trained on the timetable Pole had handed her.

She gave it a quick scan. All seemed in order. Math—Bent, Science—Bent, Music—Pagliacci, Physical Education—Mandala, Visual Arts—Washington, English—

Wait. What was this? Was Kallie seeing correctly? She adjusted her glasses and looked again, but the words were there, plain and simple. How could this be?

"As you can see," said Mr. Bent, "we have more rotation this year. The staff thought it best that I teach science and math for various classes, seeing as they are my specialties, and I am the very best . . ." He paused as though accepting an award. "While Ms. Beausoleil will teach you English."

Kallie's heart deflated like a punctured beach ball. Not Ms. Beausoleil. Anyone but Beausoleil.

"What a lovely name," whispered Anna. "Beau . . . soleil. It means *beautiful sun* in French. She must be quite stunning."

Kallie cast the girl a sour sideways glance. Whatever Anna Glud was picturing, she had a surprise coming her way.

DARK WATERS

Kallie spent the rest of the school day receiving textbooks, organizing her locker (she brought a magnetic whiteboard, a pencil holder, a mirror, an additional shelf, and a gray rubber mat for the bottom), and, most important, dodging Anna.

At least Ms. Beausoleil's class had been canceled because of orientation assembly. Kallie wouldn't have to face that unpleasantness until the following day.

After school, Grandpa met her at the front of the building. On alternate days, if the weather cooperated, they would make their way down the steep-sloped sidewalks of Main Street toward the lake. It was only a short jaunt to Waterfront Park where they would sit on one of the swinging benches and have heated discussions about politics and science.

Lake Champlain was enormous. About one hundred and twenty miles long and over twelve miles across at its widest point, it was the thirteenth-largest freshwater lake in the country. Its shimmering surface covered more than four hundred square miles, and in some spots, it dropped to four hundred feet deep. It contained seventy-one islands and countless inlets and bays. On one side, the Adirondacks rose and fell like petrified waves, while on the other, the Green Mountains faded to blue.

"Any sign of Champ?" said Grandpa Jess, nudging her shoulder.

Kallie sighed.

Locals believed the lake harbored a secret—a giant, prehistoric sea monster lurking in its depths. Hundreds of eyewitnesses—beginning with the explorer Samuel de Champlain himself—claimed to have seen greenish-brown humps slithering through the dark waters. Travelers and tourists pumped loads of money into the local economy just trying to catch a glimpse.

Grandpa Jess liked to tease Kallie about the creature. Probably to distract her, because he knew every time she looked out at the lake, she was keeping her eye out as well—though for something entirely different. The lake held secrets all right. Only, for Kallie, they had nothing to do with Champ.

Grandpa Jess was a retired fisherman. When he was young, the fish from Lake Champlain were safer to eat. Now, with higher mercury levels from coal-burning utilities and municipal waste incineration, plus microbeads—tiny plastic particles from beauty products flushed down drains—many species were no longer edible.

With only two marinas in the area, dockage was extremely limited. Wait lists could take as long as ten years. Grandpa was lucky to have a dock slip at Perkins Pier, where he kept a small boat, the *Escape*, moored. To him, fishing wasn't just a job or a sport—it was a way of life. It was in his blood. He always said that he was born an angler and that he'd be an angler until the day he died. It was also how he met Grandma Gem.

Geneviève Bonenfant came from a fishing family

in Quebec. According to Grandpa Jess, one day, when Grandma was sixteen, she had ventured out alone into the Richelieu River. A powerful wind had driven her into Lake Champlain. Her small boat was jostled perilously. Grandpa had noticed her in distress and had rescued her. Kallie's father often corrected him, stating that the Richelieu River actually flows north out of Lake Champlain and that it was, in fact, Grandma Gem who had noticed Grandpa Jess in distress and had fought the current to rescue him and not the other way around.

In any case, the two had fallen in love instantly, had gotten married, and never fought about anything other than who produced more maple syrup and who won the War of 1812. There was a festival across the lake every year commemorating the Battle of Plattsburgh. Grandpa and Grandma took part in the reenactment—on opposing sides.

Unfortunately, Kallie remembered as little about Grandma Gem as she did about The Writer. She watched a dragonfly skim the water's surface. Its blue-green body shimmered in the late-afternoon light.

All the while, Grandpa Jess fired a barrage of

questions at her. How was the first day? How did it all go? Who was her teacher? Did she find her classroom okay? How was Pole? Her other classmates? What was her locker assignment? What did she do during recess?

There was little wind, and few sailboats on the lake that day. A lone Jet Ski zigzagged in the distance, forcing curtains of water to rise up around it. Tiny waves rippled out and lapped gently and mesmerizingly against the rocks.

After a good half hour, it was time to leave. They passed the ECHO center with its bright lettering: *Ecology, Culture, History, Opportunity*. Kallie knew everything there was to know about the seventy species of fish, amphibians, invertebrates, and reptiles housed in the aquarium. She couldn't wait until tenth grade, when she could apply for an internship in the facility.

When they arrived home, Kallie's after-school snack awaited her in a white bowl on the kitchen table: an orange sliced into exactly six equal wedges. Grandpa Jess sat across from her, continuing to quiz her on her day. Once he had exhausted all questions, they sat for some time in silence.

Kallie finished her snack, and her fingers were

sticky with juice. She opened and closed them, frowning hard, until finally she broke the silence.

"Tell me more about the day *The Wri*—" She stopped, took a deep breath, and continued, "The day my *mother* drowned." She winced, the words sharp in her throat.

Grandpa's smile melted, and the warm light ever present in his eyes dimmed. He volleyed glances between the clock and Kallie, biting his lower lip. Then, finally, he responded, "All I know is what your father told me."

A shadow appeared in the kitchen doorway. Her father had come home early. They hadn't heard him enter. "And what exactly have I told you?"

Grandpa jolted. He spun round to face Kallie's father.

"Um, er . . . to make sure Kallie washes her hands before and after eating. You always say that, Victor. Now, go wash your hands, Kallie." He wagged a scolding finger. "Just like your father always says."

Victor Jones narrowed his eyes, as though not utterly convinced that had been the topic of conversation. His gaze swung like a pendulum from Grandpa

Jess to Kallie, then back to Grandpa. "I suppose I do say that."

Kallie's expression remained deadpan. She stood, lifted her bowl, and walked to the sink. Grandpa Jess wasn't lying. Though, he wasn't being entirely truthful, either. It made Kallie uneasy, but she didn't want to get him in trouble.

"Can you please turn on the faucet, Grandpa? I don't want to get it sticky."

Grandpa Jess scrambled to his feet. "Of course." His face was pale, as though he'd been caught doing something awful.

Kallie washed and dried her hands. When she was clean, her father gave her a gentle hug. "How was your day? Plenty of learning, I hope?"

Kallie smiled and nodded. She checked her watch. "Speaking of learning . . . It's homework time," she said cheerfully as she strolled past her grandfather and out of the kitchen. She picked up the satchel she'd left at the foot of the stairs and went straight to her room.

Mr. Bent had begun the term with a chapter on ordering and comparing large numbers. Even the word problems were simple for Kallie, who worked at them almost absentmindedly.

When she was finished, she picked up her text on quantum physics. She delved cheerfully into the world of subatomic particles, to which Pole had introduced her. Yet, as hard as she tried to stop her brain from wandering, it headed again and again down the dark path leading to *The Writer*.

Kallie put down the textbook. She stared at the faded photograph in the plain brass frame for a whole five minutes before she reached for it. She traced a finger around the blurry face. The woman wore an apron with something embroidered on the top. The child clutching the woman's hand was little more than a jagged-haired blob in a pale-green jacket.

As far as Kallie was concerned, the woman might have been anyone. She couldn't recall the sound of her voice, the smell of her skin, or the touch of her hand. She was a patchwork doll stitched together from the thread and fabric of other people's memories.

The two stood outside a local store—the Dollar Basket. Kallie examined the logo—a brown basket with a handle made of dollar signs. It may have been the same image embroidered on the apron, though it was tough to tell.

Kallie was three years old when her mother drowned. The facts in the case were quite simple.

One summer day, just over nine years ago, Grandpa Jess was watching Kallie when her father and mother took the car ferry to Plattsburgh. It had been very windy, and the water had been quite choppy.

Despite the captain's warnings, her mother had exited the car to gaze out at the stormy lake. Apparently, she loved writing poetry about dark, restless waters and wanted inspiration.

Kallie's father had remained in the car with his seat belt fastened the entire trip. He said he found the ferry unnerving even when the lake was calm. He preferred to take the interstate around the lake, but it was her mother who had insisted they take the ferry that day. The last he saw of her, she was headed up the stairs to the bridge.

It was a short ride—only about fifteen minutes—but when the ferry docked on the other side of the lake and all the cars had rolled off, Kallie's mother was nowhere to be found. After an extensive search-

and-rescue operation, the police ruled the incident an accidental drowning.

Kallie didn't miss her mother—not really—because, as she often said, you can't miss something you don't recall ever having. Still, she was curious. She had many unanswered questions.

Had her mother slipped? Had she been knocked over by a rogue wave? Why had they been going to Plattsburgh? But even at a very young age, she knew the subject was strictly off-limits.

Though her father never said it out loud, Kallie was sure he blamed her mother's dreamy nature for her death. If she hadn't gotten out of the car to study the water that day, she wouldn't have drowned.

"Stories are ugly little lies wrapped in pretty packages," her father said to her one day when she was four years old. She'd come home from preschool and told him her teacher had read the class the story of the three little pigs.

"They are full of promise, designed to draw you in." He picked her up, sat her on his lap, and gazed at her with deep brown eyes. "But in the end, you discover they are nothing but empty words that will break your heart. Stick to facts, Kallie. Cold, hard facts never let you down."

He set her on her feet, brushed something out of his eye, and went straight to the store. He came home with a book called *Wolves: Behavior, Habitat, and Conservation*, which he read to her in its entirety that evening.

"Wolves can't speak," Kallie told her teacher the very next day after the man began reading *Little Red Riding Hood*.

"No, they can't," the teacher had tried to explain. "Not in real life, Kallie. But this is different. This is a story."

"Daddy says if it's not true, then it's a lie."

The teacher glanced at the rest of the children, who seemed to be eagerly awaiting his response. "Things aren't always that simple . . ."

"Are you saying wolves *can* speak?" she asked.

He shook his head slowly.

"Then it's not the truth," she proclaimed proudly.

He leaned in close and spoke softly. "The truth is a slippery little worm. Be careful. It can wriggle away from you."

"Actually, worms don't wriggle," said a small boy with flat brown hair. "They use bristles as anchors. They push themselves forward or backward by stretching and contracting."

Kallie smiled at the boy. His name was Napoleon, but she decided Pole was much more efficient. From that day on, she and Pole were a team. They listened critically and with overenthusiastic skepticism to everything anyone—including teachers—told them.

Kallie placed the photograph back in its spot in the top corner of her shelf. The book on wolves her father had given her all those years ago was just below it. She had read it several times, memorizing every fact.

Everything she had learned about wolves said they were friendly, loyal, and highly intelligent creatures— just like their cuddly canine relatives. They rarely attacked humans.

Kallie thought about the creature that had glared at her the previous night. Whatever it was, it was smaller than a wolf, with a narrow, pointy muzzle and razor-sharp teeth. Its wiry coat was pearly white. And it had glowing eyes.

Except for its color, it could have been a fox. Or a jackal. And now that she thought of it, it looked similar to the sharp-eared animal carved onto the face of the first cube. She sighed. That picture must have fueled her imagination. Just as her father had said. The box was trouble.

Voices drifted into Kallie's room through the door left slightly ajar. She could hear her father and grandfather talking in hushed whispers. Kallie closed her wolf book and crept to the door. She opened it farther and put her ear to the crack. She caught snippets of conversation.

". . . not right . . ." said Grandpa Jess.

Mumble. Mumble. Mumble.

". . . did it for Kallie's sake . . ." said her father.

More muttering.

What wasn't right? Kallie wondered. What had her father done? She strained her ears, but their voices were low and foggy, and all she could snatch from them were more garbled syllables. She was about to step into the hall when something in her room made a hollow *thunk*.

Kallie swung round, half expecting the pink-eyed

creature to be leaping toward her. At first, she saw nothing out of place, but then her gaze settled on her desk and her vision narrowed to a fine point.

Sitting atop her math textbook was the box. It was turned so that the two stars were on top of the waning crescent moon, making it look like two eyes and a mouth. It was grinning at her.

7

A BEAUTIFUL SUN

"Welcome to Narnia!" announced a broad, hunched woman of gargantuan stature.

She had rust-colored hair; green eyes set so wide and low they nearly aligned with her ears; crooked, coffee-stained teeth; and a chin pointy enough to spear pineapple. Her billowing white dress was a sort of cross between a karate gi and a bathrobe.

Kallie peeked inside the third-floor classroom and sighed. It was worse than she'd expected. There wasn't a single desk. Instead, the room was filled with truckloads of worn pillows most likely salvaged from a yard sale. Plush ones, floral ones, striped and polka dot. Cotton, chenille, and faux fur.

This wasn't a classroom, Kallie decided. At best,

it was a giant slumber party. At worst, a fire hazard. She made a mental list of all the building-code violations. She would notify Mr. McEwan just as soon as she saw him.

"In you go," said Ms. Beausoleil. "Make yourselves comfortable."

Kallie planted her feet, rooting them firmly to the old tiles. Everyone, including Anna, rushed past her on either side. They practically dove onto the pillows, stretching themselves out, shouting and laughing in a most unruly manner.

"Hello, Kaliope," said Ms. Beausoleil.

"Kallie," she replied softly. "Not Kaliope."

The teacher tilted her head and smiled apologetically.

"Where are the desks?" asked Kallie. "How are we supposed to work?"

"Oh, we are going to work very hard, I can assure you," said Ms. Beausoleil. "But you won't need a desk. Not here." She tilted her head side to side. "Well, not at the moment, anyway."

"But how are we supposed to write about our studies?" Kallie protested.

"Write *about* our studies?" Ms. Beausoleil seemed genuinely confused. "We aren't going to merely write about the stories we study. We are going to *live* them. *Breathe* them. Let them take hold of our very souls and spirit us away." She appeared to clutch at something in the air and then cast it off toward a distant horizon. She grinned and winked.

Kallie narrowed her eyes and clenched her jaw as the teacher gently guided her inside. She reluctantly crossed the threshold.

"This is an affront to education," she muttered under her breath. "It's anarchy."

"Not to mention unhygienic," whispered Pole, who came marching in behind.

"Now, now," said Ms. Beausoleil. "Speak up. No whisperings or mutterings necessary here. I encourage free conversation, differing opinions, and debate in my classroom."

Kallie made a pinched face while Pole carefully cleared a spot on the dusty, tiled floor. He sat cross-legged. Kallie remained standing. The very idea of working in such close proximity to other people's messy thoughts upset her. They'd be like sticky fingers reaching over and messing with her mind.

Once everyone had settled, Ms. Beausoleil reached behind her, grabbed a worn book from one of the numerous dusty stacks piled high at the front of the class, and held it up for all to see. Its cover was wrinkled and cracked, its pages yellow, and the corners dog-eared.

"*The Lion, the Witch and the Wardrobe*," she said. "A hero's journey. A tale of courage and sacrifice. Betrayal and redemption. Fraught with consequence and award-winning pain. Filled with magic." She smiled. "Ah, yes . . . magic."

Anna sat up straighter. Her face beamed like a lighthouse. Kallie sighed. Just what she needed. More magic.

"Written first, this novel is actually the second book in the series. The sixth book is the first, the fifth is the third, the second the fourth, and—"

Kallie shook her head. Any writer who couldn't decide on the sequence of events was simply not to be trusted.

"Today, you are no longer students." Ms. Beausoleil eyed half the room. "You are dryads and nymphs." She nodded at the other half and smiled. "Red dwarfs and fauns."

Kallie observed her classmates. Their eyes widened with curiosity. Even the cool kids who worked very hard at appearing perpetually bored seemed a little intrigued.

Then Ms. Beausoleil's gaze settled on Kallie. "Have a seat, dear." She motioned to a large, lumpy pillow with a paisley pattern.

"I prefer to stand," said Kallie, unable to mask the disdain in her voice.

"Wonderful!" said Ms. Beausoleil. "We shall need a lamp-post as well!"

Kallie could feel steam rising from her skull as the teacher settled onto her own pillow the size of a truck tire. And with a great sigh blowing through the class like dry wind across the desert, she began to read:

"*Once there were four children whose names were Peter, Susan, Edmund, and Lucy.*"

Kallie stared at the clock above the door. She

watched the second hand *tick*, *tick*, *tick* as the wasted period dwindled. All the while, she tried desperately to tune out the story. It wormed its way into her head all the same.

It made no sense. A world through a wardrobe? Ridiculous—not to mention scientifically impossible.

At long last, a bell sounded, putting Kallie out of her misery. Ms. Beausoleil had managed to read five chapters. All four children had now entered the wardrobe and were left shut in the dark.

"That's it for today," said Ms. Beausoleil, closing the book.

"No!" shouted Alex.

"You can't leave us hanging!" squeaked Grace.

Ms. Beausoleil sat grinning as the class moaned, groaned, and begged her to continue. "Tomorrow you must come prepared—for the road ahead is perilous. And I will call upon each of you to take a turn reading."

Accepting the period was over, everyone gathered their belongings, chatting happily about the story as they left the class.

"Isn't she beautiful?" whispered Anna as she passed Kallie.

"I suppose . . . if you like gerenuks." Kallie sighed. How would she ever survive the year? If only she could have had Mr. Bent. She'd heard the previous sixth graders had spent the entire year diagramming sentences. Kallie was an expert in pronouns, verbs, articles, and adjectives. She knew her subjective completions and subordinate clauses like the back of her hand. She eyed Pole, and a silent message passed between them.

"Lunchtime," he said.

Aside from math and science, it was Pole's favorite time of day. Kallie sanitized her hands three times, retrieved her lunch bag from her locker, and followed Pole into the cafeteria.

By the time they arrived, many of the long tables were occupied. They found an empty end and sat opposite each other.

Pole got out his thermos filled with a thick, lentilish mush. He was a strict vegetarian. Kallie sanitized her hands one more time for good measure and then began to munch on a cucumber and salmon sandwich. She had sliced the cucumbers extrathin and cut the bread diagonally, just the way she liked it.

"How could they all fit in the wardrobe?" said Pole. "It's not physically possible."

"It's magic, remember," said Kallie, sarcasm distorting her expression.

"Magic! I know everything there is to know about magic!" trilled the now-familiar and all-too-enthusiastic voice. Anna hovered over them, her backpack slung over her shoulder, a chipped ceramic cup dangling between her fingers. "Didn't I tell you?"

"Tell us what?" asked Pole.

Kallie fired him an angry look. Pole should know better than to encourage the girl. She was one of those people with permanently rosy cheeks. It made her look excessively cheerful all the time. Of course, cheerfulness had its place, thought Kallie. But it was a small space, a neat and tidy compartment between joy and contentment. Anna's cheerfulness was sloppy. It spilled all over the place, dripping onto the floor, leaving a trail of smiles wherever she went. Disgusting.

Anna slipped onto the bench beside Kallie. "My

parents are world-famous magicians. They've traveled the globe with the Curious Carnival of Kickapoo Kansas, performing for all sorts of nobility. Kings . . . queens . . . basketball stars . . . Perhaps you've heard of them? The Amazing Alonzo and his Alluring Assistant, Ava."

Pole shook his head while Kallie sat blinking.

"Well, no matter. Maybe someday you'll come see their show. When they're back, that is."

"Listen," said Pole, changing topics. "I've been thinking. I'm tired of all the silly celebrations we are forced to endure. Halloween, Valentine's Day, Groundhog Day . . ."

"The worst, because it pretends to be scientific." Kallie nodded.

"So," he continued, "this year, I think our school should celebrate something truly meaningful."

Kallie could see the glint in Pole's eyes. He rarely got this excited about anything. She knew something great was coming.

"National Periodic Table Day." He raised his chin in triumph.

Kallie beamed. Anna looked confused. "National what day?"

"Periodic table," said Kallie. "Pay attention."

"National Periodic Table Day," said Pole, "occurs every February seventh to promote the challenges overcome by individuals in order to create the modern periodic table."

"I love the idea! It's cooler than absolute zero," said Kallie.

Pole grinned.

"How are we supposed to celebrate that?" said Anna.

"Well," said Pole, "I was thinking we could begin by playing the periodic table song, then cycle through various chemistry challenges and . . ."

"Hey—why did the scientist dip his shoes in silicone rubber?" said Kallie.

"To reduce his carbon footprint," said Pole. They giggled.

"I've got an idea!" announced Anna. "We can all come dressed as our favorite element."

Kallie stopped laughing and stared.

"Well," said Pole, "how about we put that in the maybe box."

"I'm going to come as Kryptonite," she said with a smugness Kallie felt was utterly unearned.

"It's krypton," said Kallie. "There's no such thing as Kryptonite."

"Not on this planet," said Anna. "Why should I limit myself to earthly elements?"

"There's no Kryptonite on any planet," said Kallie, increasingly annoyed.

"How do you know?" said Anna. "Have you mapped the entire universe?"

"She has a point, Kallie." Pole smiled at Anna, then ate a big spoonful of mush.

Kallie gritted her teeth. She didn't know what galled her more—Anna's ridiculousness or Pole's defense of it. She took a bite of her sandwich, all the while eyeing the girl's backpack and her ceramic cup. It looked hand-painted, with splotches of purple and green covering the inside and out. On the front was a single, lopsided pink heart. "Where's your lunch?"

"Oh, I had an absolutely ginormous breakfast.

Mrs. Winslow—I'm living with her while my parents are away—makes the biggest breakfasts in the world. A veritable smorgasbord of sausages, bacon, and ham. Pancakes shaped like flowers with whipped cream petals. And the fluffiest scrambled eggs that just melt in your mouth. I'm really stuffed, couldn't eat another bite."

She paused for a quick breath. "But . . . I would like some water. Where is the nearest fountain?" She plunked her backpack on the bench next to Kallie and held up her cup.

Pole pointed to the hallway. "Just outside the cafeteria, in front of the washroom. I can show you the way."

"No need," said Anna. "I'll be right back."

"What do you think of her?" he asked once Anna was out of earshot. He was smiling again—as if he'd just received an A+ on an assignment.

"I try not to," said Kallie. She shifted away from the musty-smelling, shabby-looking backpack crammed with so much stuff it was coming apart at the seams.

"I don't know. I kind of like her."

"How can you?" said Kallie indignantly. "She's so . . . incongruent."

"Yes." He nodded. "I think that's it. There's a sort of scalene quality about her, don't you think?"

Kallie rolled her eyes and sighed. She took another bite of her sandwich, chewed, and swallowed, all the while thinking. "Can I ask you something?" she said finally.

"Is it about geometry?" he said, eagerly.

Kallie shook her head. She chose her words carefully. "Have you ever done something, well, without thinking?"

Pole nearly dropped his spoon. He looked shocked. "You mean something rash? Impulsive? *Unplanned?*"

"No, no. Nothing like that," she said, her cheeks turning pink. "What I meant to say was, have you ever, well, done something, such as gotten something out of the fridge without knowing you'd done so? Maybe you poured yourself a glass of milk without realizing and the next thing you knew it was sitting on the counter waiting for you and you had no idea you'd done it? Like that?"

Kallie pictured the box, sitting on her desk, as though she had placed it there herself when she was certain she hadn't gone near it.

"Of course I have," said Pole. He pointed his spoon at her. "You're talking about the automatic brain."

"The *automatic brain*?"

"Exactly." Pole dug into his thermos, extracted a heaping spoonful of mush, placed it in his mouth, and swished it around for a bit before swallowing.

"You see, most of what we do everyday, we do unconsciously—without thinking about it. Our brain has memorized patterns of behavior, and then we just go through the motions."

Kallie let the idea swish around her brain like a glob of Pole's mush. It made sense. She could have gotten out the box unconsciously.

"If we had to think about every single movement, every single breath, every single step, or blink, or cough," said Pole, "we'd be exhausted. Thinking is really hard work."

"So, it's as though we go on autopilot?" said Kallie, placing the remainder of her sandwich into the tupperware and zipping up her lunch bag.

"It's the magic of the unconscious mind!" said Anna, shifting her backpack down the bench, slipping in beside Kallie, placing her cup on the table.

Kallie had no idea Anna had been there, eavesdropping on their conversation. She was about to tell Anna there was no such thing as magic when she heard a loud *crash* and the cafeteria went silent.

8

THE GOBLET

Liah's eyelids fluttered open, and her arms fell limp at her sides. She was standing alone. If there had been a beast, she had frightened it away.

She was about to turn back when, in the distance, her eyes caught a faint glimmer. Curious, she wove through the labyrinth of tree trunks toward it. When at last she passed through a thick patch of brush and came upon the source, the breath caught in her throat.

Scattered about the ground as far as she could see lay a mass of bones—so many they would be impossible to count. It was a strange and mystifying sight. The bone carver had said the forest was haunted by the spirits of those who had no ancestors to provide them with a proper burial—but surely he did not mean their bones had been merely discarded here like so much rubble?

Liah reached out a trembling hand and picked up the piece closest to her. It was a skull, cold and smooth and so white it shone silver. How strange, she thought, for bone preparation was a lengthy process. A bone must be boiled three times, and then a fourth using a washing powder before it can lie in the sun to bleach white.

The bone she held was such a fine piece. She could carve from it a weaving tool, or a cloak pin, many charms or buttons to sell in the village market. She wondered if perhaps the bone carver came to this place in secret to obtain his bones. Perhaps that was why he bade her stick to the path.

Liah withdrew a piece of cloth from her sack, wrapped the skull, and slipped it into her satchel, promising herself she would perform the rituals to release the spirit once she was home. The bone carver would be less angry once he beheld all the lovely items she had created from it.

As she turned to leave, she stood searching in one direction, then another, but could no longer see the path whence she had come. The forest around her seemed darker and deeper, as though it might go on forever. She had wandered farther than she had thought.

Liah began to pick a careful path in one direction, but after several paces, she determined she was mistaken. She turned and tried another. Overhanging branches knit above, reaching down with blackened, brittle fingers. As she made her way through the forest, all the tree trunks began to look familiar, as though she were wandering in circles.

"Master!" she called, but her voice was dull and refused to carry. Her heart beat a rhythm in her throat as she tried again, this time louder and more fervently: "Master!"

From somewhere behind her, she heard a soft sound. Her insides tingled with unease. If the white beast had returned, it might not scare again so easily. She uprooted herself and began to run.

Liah dashed as fast as her feet could manage, dodging trees and branches, but it was as though the forest were collapsing in around her, swallowing her in its dark folds. She imagined a soft murmur of voices rising up from somewhere in the distance, moving toward her, drawing nearer.

She paused for only a brief moment to catch her breath and search for direction. She spun round and round, dizzying herself, when suddenly a hand gripped her shoulder. The voices stopped.

"What has happened? Why did you cry out?"

Relief washed over Liah as the bone carver steadied her in his strong but gentle arms.

"I-I became lost. And something gave chase." Her voice faltered. She pointed to a spot behind the nearest trunk. "A beast," she said breathlessly. "A white beast." She scanned every shadow, but nothing stirred. All was silent.

The bone carver's gaze slipped from Liah's eyes to her feet. She stood once again by the animal bones she had first come upon. It was as though she had not moved from the spot.

He released his grip and scowled. "I warned you not to disturb anything in this forest. You have disobeyed."

Liah hung her head. She could not find any words to argue. He held her gaze—long enough for shame to settle into her stomach—and then he turned and headed back toward the path. She scrambled after him, scolding herself for not having heeded his warning.

When they reached the edge of the woods, the bone carver stooped to retrieve his sack. He must have cast it aside when he had come running to find her. It lay against a jagged rock. As he inspected his goods, his frown hardened. His most precious carving had been damaged.

Liah took the goblet from his hands. The intricate patterns had taken much time to carve, and the turquoise inlay had cost five coppers. He had spent countless days polishing it until it gleamed. Now the side was scraped, its value cheapened.

"Your foolishness has angered the ancestors," he said.

Liah rubbed the scratches with her thumb, hoping they would disappear, but no matter how hard she pressed, the damage remained. She knew her master could no longer present the cup to the Empress. It had been his most valuable piece. If he had sold it, they would have had food for many seasons.

"When we arrive at the palace, you will remain outside," he said firmly.

The words struck Liah like a hand across the face. She had never been allowed to accompany him to the palace. When he agreed to take her, she boasted to all the villagers how she would see the inner courtyard and the great stone terrace with her own eyes.

Pleading would be of no use. The bone carver was a kind and thoughtful man, but once he set a punishment, it was as though he had carved it in bone.

She took a scrap of cloth from her provisions sack and carefully wrapped the goblet. As she placed it inside, she remembered the skull she had taken from the forest. She should go back and return it, but how could she do so without the bone carver's knowledge? She resolved to keep it safely hidden. She would find an opportunity to return the skull to the forest on the journey home.

9

FRAGMENTS AND SHARDS

The cup lay on the floor in two pieces. The handle had broken off. A puddle spread out around the cup as though it were bleeding water. Pole and Anna and all the nearby students eyed Kallie solemnly.

"Why did you do that?" said Anna quietly. It was not an accusation, but a simple question.

Kallie's cheeks blazed. Her gaze volleyed from one pair of eyes to another. "I-I didn't," she stammered. She shuffled off the bench and stooped to pick up the pieces. "I don't know what happened. But I didn't touch your cup . . ."

Her voice trailed off as she looked toward Pole for reassurance, but he merely winced and then nodded as if to confirm Anna's accusation.

Kallie couldn't understand it. She hadn't laid a finger on the cup. She was sure of it . . . absolutely certain of it . . . *wasn't she*? Had she knocked it down accidentally without realizing? Or had her limbs somehow reacted independently of her thoughts? The automatic brain? Again she looked toward Pole, but his expression was draped in worry.

Something was happening. Something Kallie couldn't explain. Not even to herself. "I'm sorry," she said, lifting the pieces, still unconvinced of her guilt.

Anna smiled. "Don't worry." She took the cup from Kallie, cradling the two pieces gently. "Objects, unlike people, can be easily repaired." Her eyes remained as bright as beacons, though her lower lip quivered slightly.

Kallie swallowed a large lump growing in her throat. "Is there anything I can do?"

Anna placed the shards on the table, reached for her worn purple backpack, and located a small bottle of glue. "Well," she said, cheerfulness flooding steadily back into her voice. "If you're not going to eat the other half of that sandwich . . ."

"But . . ." said Kallie, "I thought you said you were too stuffed to eat?"

"I am. Really." Anna placed small dabs of glue on the cup where the handle belonged. "But . . . well, I'd hate to see good food go to waste." She smiled.

Kallie glanced at Pole, who shrugged, finishing the last of his mush.

She unzipped her lunch bag and retrieved the half sandwich from the untouched tupperware. One side was squished, and a slice of cucumber had slipped out and lay at the bottom of the container. She handed it to Anna, who accepted it graciously.

Pole gathered his belongings and stood. "We have math next. I don't want to be late. I hear Mr. Bent bought new protractors."

Kallie took a deep breath. Math class. With shiny new protractors. The day was not completely lost.

———————————— •◦• ————————————

During math, Mr. Bent instructed the class in calculating the area of obtuse triangles. Kallie completed her task well ahead of everyone—including Pole.

As she sat waiting, she thought about the cup, and

something niggled inside her. Like a blurry face on the other side of damp, foggy glass. Unclear. Distorted. She couldn't quite see it. Not yet. But she could feel it there, waiting for her.

Out of the corner of her eye, Kallie noticed Anna struggling. Kallie reached over and sketched a dotted line, creating the angle necessary for Anna to solve the equation.

"Thanks," whispered Anna, but Kallie quickly looked away, pretending she hadn't heard.

When Kallie had picked up Anna's cup, she'd seen a word on the bottom—painted with jagged and uneven strokes: *Mom*. Had the cup been a gift from Anna to her mother? Perhaps a birthday or Mother's Day present?

Kallie had once made her father a set of coasters from old, mismatched tiles her teacher must have gotten from a thrift store. The children had each painted them and wrapped them in tissue paper for Father's Day.

Kallie took her gift home and waited excitedly as her father unpacked it. He smiled and said thank you, but he worried the tiles would scratch the table. A week later she found them in the garbage.

Would She *have done the same?* Kallie wondered. Would *She* have kept Kallie's gift? Perhaps Anna's mother was like Kallie's father. Maybe she saw no use for such an unattractive cup.

A cup. A broken cup . . .

Something continued to trouble Kallie's mind. Like fragments and shards of an image smashed and scattered about the floor of her brain. She would only piece them together the following day in music class.

10

A HAUNTING MELODY

Mr. Pagliacci adjusted his collar. He had an assortment of shirts with swashbuckling necklines. They might have made him look a little like a pirate, but with his hanging jowls, droopy eyes, and red bulbous nose, he reminded Kallie more of a sad—slightly intoxicated—clown.

"This year, vocal music has given way to instrumental," he proclaimed with both pride and enthusiasm.

Kallie's stomach clenched. Her singing voice was like sandpaper grating against glass. But play an instrument? How would she ever manage? She wouldn't be allowed to practice—that was certain. Her father didn't even like to listen to well-played music. He'd never stand for subperfect screechings, ornery honk-ings, and tuneless tootings.

"Now, it is my firm belief," said Mr. Pagliacci, his forehead creased with concern, "that it is the moral and ethical duty of a good music teacher to place each student with the instrument on which they will have the highest probability of success . . ."

Kallie cast Pole an anxious glance. On the probability scale, with one being certain and zero being impossible, she gauged her instrumental success at 0.1—in words, highly unlikely.

And now, not only would she have to suffer through another half hour of instrumental agony, it would be followed by a double period of Ms. Beausoleil and then a long, languid weekend. She couldn't understand why the state of Vermont insisted on beginning school before Labor Day. Three days of school. Then three days off. Inconsistency was the main ingredient in the recipe for failure.

". . . Therefore, rather than have you choose by some whimsical fancy, such as *I like the color—the shape*—I shall assign you your instruments. The key to success is a perfect match."

Mr. Pagliacci retrieved a clipboard from beneath the reams of sheet music and books cluttering his desk and had everyone line up, facing him. It seemed a bit odd—though nothing artistic people did made any sense to Kallie. To her, *creative* was synonymous with *unpredictable* and a hairbreadth from *unstable*.

"Jonah Abercrombie," began the teacher, scrutinizing the first student. "Yes. Yes. Reasonably straight teeth, medium lips—perfect for the embouchure—long, thin fingers . . ." He jotted something on his clipboard and then shouted, startling everyone, "Flute!"

Mr. Pagliacci went on to assign Queenie Choy the clarinet because of her short, wide fingers; Ivan Gruzinsky the saxophone for his height and robustness; and Saif Khan the trombone as, according to Mr. Pagliacci, he had particularly long arms.

All three appeared offended, and though Mr. Pagliacci's observations were not altogether inaccurate, Kallie decided thick fingers, a wide girth, and Neanderthal arms weren't all too complimentary.

Kallie was up next. She planted her feet firmly and glared at the teacher. Were her lips too thin? Did she have crocodile arms? She steeled herself, but Mr. Pagliacci glanced at her for a mere fraction of a second before scribbling something onto his clipboard. He looked up briefly, smiled, and said one word.

"Triangle."

The triangle. Kallie seethed. How dare he? It was dismissive. Bordering on insulting. And yet . . . perfectly equilateral, not to mention required little practice. She settled nicely into the idea once Pole was given the cymbals—only a slight step above her in the percussion pecking order.

Musical relationships are nothing more than mathematical relationships, Kallie reassured herself. Fractions . . . simple ratios . . . patterns . . .

Nearly all the instruments had been allocated when Mr. Pagliacci arrived in front of Anna. Before he could examine her or say a word, she pulled something out from her backpack.

"This is my instrument," she said decisively. She held out an odd whitish lump riddled with holes.

Kallie stood in silent amusement, fully expecting a swift reprimand for such insolence, but instead, Mr. Pagliacci's eyes grew wide, and the corners of his mouth curled into what appeared to be, of all things, delight.

"Why, it's a vessel flute—an ocarina," he said gently, his eyes twinkling.

"An oca-who?" asked Jonah.

"An ocarina," said Anna. "It's an ancient instrument. Over twelve thousand years old. The Mayans and the Aztecs made them. So did the ancient Chinese."

"In China, it's called a *xun*," said Queenie.

"Yes—a xun," repeated Anna, "and in Italy they call it an ocarina, *little goose*, because it looks like a goose egg. This one's made from bone."

"A bone flute?" said Ivan.

"As in real bone?" said Saif.

Taylor recoiled. "That's disgusting."

"It's exquisite," said Mr. Pagliacci. "Tell me, Anna, can you play?"

She grinned and nodded. Then she placed her fingers—*not too thick, not too thin*, thought Kallie—on the holes of the gourdlike instrument and blew gently over the mouthpiece.

A soft, heavy note combining high pitch and low

pitch in perfect harmony floated out of the instrument. It was desolate and lonely and sorrowful and elegant.

As Kallie listened to the melody rise and fall, something clicked inside her brain, and her knees turned to pudding. She had heard the tune before. That night the circles had spun backward. It had come from the box.

— ❧ 11 ❧ —

THE BONE FLUTE

Liah and the bone carver had emerged from the woods just as the sun began to set. A hazy twilight ignited the air, setting the bronze fields of wild sorghum on either side of them aglow. In the distance, the road split in two, and at the fork, a small fire blazed. Behind it sat a cloaked figure.

The bone carver cast Liah a swift sideways glance. She understood the warning immediately. The Empress has many spies, *he had warned her.* Strangers were not to be trusted.

The figure made no move as the two drew near. A thin hand stretched a wooden stick over the crackling flames. On it, pieces of meat sizzled, and a rich, gamy aroma filled the air.

Liah's stomach moaned. She had eaten nothing since

the dry millet cake she had devoured before they set out. She carried only four more such cakes, two for the evening and two for morning. If the ancestors saw fit, the bone carver would sell many carvings, and they would have plenty of copper—perhaps even silver—with which to purchase provisions for the journey home. If not, they would return hungry.

The bone carver set down his sack. He cupped his hands, stretched forward, and then raised them slightly, making the traditional salute to the stranger's ancestors.

"Sit," said a deep, hollow voice. "Share the fire." The stranger motioned to other sticks and pieces of fresh meat flayed from a badger or squirrel lying atop a cloth beside him. "And the food."

If this was a trick to gain their trust, thought Liah, it was a good trick. She dropped her sack and took a step toward the sticks, but the bone carver barred her path.

"May your ancestors protect you during the day and keep watch over you by night," he said.

The figure reached up with a free hand and pulled back the hood, revealing a gaunt face, with sculpted cheeks and a ruddy mouth. It was an odd face, thought Liah. It seemed to have an ageless quality—tired, wise eyes set

deep into smooth, youthful skin that seemed to glisten in the pale moonlight.

"What sets you on this path?" asked the mysterious man.

"We head for the palace to peddle our wares," said the bone carver, seating himself next to the man, taking the stick, threading a piece of meat onto it, and holding it over the open fire. He nodded toward Liah, who quickly joined them, happy for the warm meal and the chance to rest her aching feet.

"Such coincidence," said the man. "I, too, intend to barter a trade."

Liah searched around for an indication of what the man may be selling. She could see no sack filled with items or grains. "And what might you bring to sell?"

A thin grin snaked across his lips. "Lies."

Liah bristled. She had never heard such a silly idea. It sounded neither practical nor profitable. She took a large portion of meat, threaded it onto a stick, and held it over the fire. "Who would purchase such a thing? There is no value in it."

The bone carver looked at her sharply. She closed her

mouth and bit her tongue. Insulting a gracious host was equal to insulting the ancestors.

"Ah," said the man thoughtfully. "Lies can have great value. In fact, to some they might even be a means of survival."

Liah frowned. How could a lie help a person survive? You could not wear it or eat it or wield it. She thought about this for some time, and as her meat began to sizzle, she asked, "Tell me, how does one go about selling a lie?"

The stranger's smile grew thinner still. He removed his stick from the fire, his piece of meat crusted and golden. "Why, my young friend, the best way to sell a lie is to cloak it in truth."

"That smacks of deceit," said Liah, not even attempting to hide her disdain. She removed her stick from the fire to let the crisp meat cool.

"Are we not all deceitful at one time or other?" he said. "Be it born of necessity or desire?" He held her gaze, and she imagined he could see deep inside her. As though he knew her recent deeds.

Her cheeks grew hot and radish-red. She was unsure if it was the warmth of the fire or something else. She cleared her throat. "Is that all you sell?"

"Oh no. Of course not." He chuckled. "I have a great selection of falsehoods, fibs, and fancies. Not to mention some rather clever rumors, insinuation, and innuendo. And sometimes . . ." He leaned in close, and Liah thought he smelled of clover and codfish. "For special customers only . . . I sell stories."

Lies? Rumors? Stories? What nonsense this stranger spouted. Liah opened her mouth, preparing to tell him so, when the bone carver interjected.

"Forgive the young one. She is still learning proper manners." He ate his small piece of meat and drew a hand across his mouth, slick with grease. Then he picked up Liah's sack. She flinched, worried he might find the skull she had taken from the forest and know her deception. She relaxed her tense muscles and popped the cooled meat into her mouth when he withdrew one of her carvings.

It was an odd-shaped object, hollow on the inside, with holes carved into various points. He presented it to the stranger, bowing in the sign of thanks. "Payment for your kindness."

Liah nearly choked on her piece of meat. The bone flute was her first carving. She was proud of the instrument, for though it was not all too pleasant to the eye, it made a rich sound. It was hers to sell, not the bone carver's to squander on this storyteller. This lie peddler.

The stranger bowed in the proper response and accepted the gift. "A fine piece," he said, studying it from all sides. He smiled at Liah, and then he narrowed his eyes. "Tell me, have you performed the proper rituals? Has the spirit been set free, or shall I be haunted by the cow or deer to which this bone belongs?"

How dare this man question her carving! She wished to snatch it back, but the bone carver stayed her arm.

"The rituals were obeyed," he assured the stranger. "I performed them myself. No spirit lingers in this marrow. Your dreams shall not be plagued."

Liah clenched her jaw. Her words came out tight and brittle. "May your bones one day be laid to rest and your ancestors perform the rituals to set your spirit free." It was a proper blessing to bestow upon someone, yet the bone carver cast Liah an angry look, knowing well her tone had meant otherwise.

"I do not have ancestors," said the man flatly. "And I have little interest in having my spirit set free."

Liah and the bone carver both bristled at such foolish and disrespectful words.

"Now, now. You must not fret." He waved a hand. "If my spirit were to be set free, my journey would end. And I have much more to accomplish in this world." He examined the carving in his hand again. "Truly excellent craftsmanship. Yes. Perhaps you shall be the one to help me with my journey onward."

Liah and the bone carver exchanged curious glances.

"Now," he said with a smile, "perhaps I might have something new to trade. A tune, perhaps?" He placed his fingers on the holes and began to play a hollow melody.

The night grew ripe with shadows as the purple sky faded to black. Liah sat sulking at the loss of her carving. She ate her fill, all the while listening to the low, whispery notes of the bone flute.

She did not trust this stranger who claimed to sell stories and lies, but the journey had been long, and her head grew weary. She rested it against her satchel, and though she tried to keep one eye open, she drifted off with the mournful music of the bone flute rising and falling in her dreams.

Liah awoke in darkness. The fire had turned to ash, and the bone flute lay beside her. The stranger was gone.

12

ASSIGNMENT #1

While Mr. Pagliacci busied himself assigning instruments, Kallie gathered her wits and approached Anna. "May I see that?"

Anna stopped playing. She smiled and handed Kallie the ocarina.

"This is a bone?" Kallie turned the piece over in her hands. "You're sure?"

Anna nodded. "My great-great-grandfather was an archaeologist. He excavated it from a dig in southern China. It's a real artifact."

Tsars. Magicians. Archaeologists. Anna certainly had an interestingly eclectic family.

Kallie felt the weight of the ocarina. She ran her fingers along the rutted surface. It felt like the same material as the circular inlays on the box. The same material as the pieces she'd tossed. The pieces that had landed on the same pictures three times. They must be made of bone.

Kallie handed the instrument back to Anna, who took it gently and began to play softly once again. In her mind's eye, Kallie drew three squares and in them she recalled each of the images.

An animal. A broken cup. And something strikingly similar to Anna's ocarina . . .

A prickling sense of dread settled into Kallie's stomach. Something strange was happening. Something that connected her to the box. And to the bones.

———— ·•· ————

Kallie had less patience for Ms. Beausoleil's class than the previous day. First, because the teacher wore a potato-sack-shaped dress made of gold lamé. Second, because it was last period on Friday and she desperately needed to get home to the box. She had to open it again. She had to stop whatever was happening and take back control.

To make matters worse, it was a double period, so

she grudgingly cleared a space beside Pole at the rear of the class and sat cross-legged, trying not to make contact with any unhygienic pillows, while the other students took turns reading chapter after chapter of the ridiculous story. Talking beavers. People turned to stone. Utter nonsense.

To distract herself, Kallie continued to think about the pieces that had tumbled out of the box. She had an excellent memory for detail. She could visualize each one.

The first piece had a foxlike image. And then a strange white animal had appeared outside her bedroom. The second piece had a broken cup, and then Anna's cup was smashed. The third piece—the one that looked like an egg with holes—was most decidedly an ocarina. It had to be. And then there was the music. The hollow melody that had come from the box . . . What could it all mean?

"Now," said Ms. Beausoleil, taking the novel from Queenie. Together, they had managed several more chapters, passing the halfway point. "I have an assignment for you."

The class groaned in unison.

"But it's a long weekend," whined Taylor.

"All the more time to spend on the assignment," said Ms. Beausoleil.

Taylor flopped back into her pile of pillows and continued grumbling.

"But . . ." said Mathusha. "It's Labor Day. Aren't you supposed to get time off from work?"

"To earn time *off* from work you have to spend time *on* it. Good thing you have Saturday and Sunday to warrant that holiday Monday," said Ms. Beausoleil.

Kallie wondered what sort of assignment the woman had come up with. She hoped it would not be some ridiculous imaginative adventure. Perhaps she'd be lucky, and it would be something she could handle, like a timeline of the events. Or a graph of the various creatures and how often they appeared in the story. With a little luck, a report on the improbability of the entire thing.

"You will be writing a letter," said Ms. Beausoleil.

Kallie, who only realized in that moment she'd been holding her breath, exhaled. A letter. That might be okay. She could write a letter to the author explaining her disdain for his narrative. She could write a letter to the publisher complaining of the nonsense they'd published. She could write a letter to the principal, the school board, the parent council . . .

"You will be writing the letter from the viewpoint of one of the characters," Ms. Beausoleil continued. "You may choose Lucy or Edmund."

Another person's viewpoint? Kallie could have guessed there'd be a catch to this letter-writing exercise.

"You will be writing to your mother, who is in London during World War II and who has sent you to live with your uncle and . . ."

Kallie raised her hand so sharply that had there been a balloon above her, it would have popped.

Ms. Beausoleil stopped midsentence. "Yes, Kaliope?"

"Kallie. Just Kallie."

"Yes, Kallie." The teacher corrected herself.

"Why?"

Ms. Beausoleil paused and smiled, waiting for Kallie to finish. When nothing more was added, she responded, "Why what?"

"Why do we have to write a letter as though we are one of the characters? I don't understand the purpose."

"Well . . ." said Ms. Beausoleil. "So you can learn to see things from another perspective . . . So you can demonstrate understanding of a character's feelings, viewpoint, voice . . ."

"But I have my own voice and my own viewpoint, and that's good enough for me."

Pole nodded vigorously. "Me too."

"Try the activity," said Ms. Beausoleil, her words stretching out like gentle, encouraging arms. "Perhaps you'll both discover something about yourselves you didn't know."

"I'm going to pick Edmund," said Anna when the bell sounded. She tried to poke her way between Kallie and Pole, who formed a solid wall as they left the class.

"Edmund?" said Pole. "Wouldn't it be easier for you to write as Lucy?"

Anna looked confused and annoyed. "Why would it?"

"Isn't it obvious?" said Pole, blushing.

Kallie rolled her eyes.

"Because I'm a girl?" snapped Anna. "That's pretty narrow-minded. Besides, a writer can become whomever they wish. I can be a boy. Or a girl. Or a moth. Or an alien trapped in a human body I'd invaded and then somehow gotten stuck in and left behind by my interstellar exploration mission—"

"Have a good weekend, Pole," interrupted Kallie. She took several paces and then stopped. Without looking back, she added, with more feeling than she'd intended, "You too, Anna." She marched straight to her locker and out the building.

———— · • · ————

"I don't want to go to the lake today."

Grandpa Jess appeared startled. "Why? Is something wrong?"

"No," she said, not being entirely truthful.

"Are you sure? It's a disruption to your schedule."

Kallie hadn't thought about her schedule all day. She became all the more convinced there *was* something wrong, something very wrong, but she tried to rationalize her feelings. "I have a lot of math and science homework. Plus an English assignment."

Grandpa Jess eyed her for a judgmental moment and then shrugged. "You know best. Schoolwork comes first."

As they walked, Grandpa Jess asked his usual questions, and Kallie responded absentmindedly, her thoughts drifting from the conversation to the box. She couldn't tell Grandpa about the strange coincidences between the images and the happenings. After all, they were just coincidences, and he might think she was becoming *imaginative*. She shuddered at the idea.

Once home, Kallie ignored her snack and went straight to her room. The box was on her shelf where she'd left it. The side facing her had two stars atop the last quarter of the moon. This time, it looked like a large, toothy smile.

She sat at her desk, frowning at the box for the longest time before she reached for it. If she could open it and see the pieces again . . . If she could just hear the melody one more time, to be absolutely sure . . .

Getting out her notepad, Kallie looked up the moves she'd recorded. But when she tried to manipulate the circles, they wouldn't budge, as though the mechanism had been broken. Or as though the box no longer wanted to be opened.

Kallie thought about the pictures on the bones once again. The jackal. The broken cup. The ocarina. She set the box down and pressed her memory. Next came a castle, a flaming cylinder, and then a coffin . . .

She looked up at the box. It continued to smile.

13

Gone Fishing

The water was as dark as a dreamless night. A large full moon lit the rippled surface, turning it to black beveled glass. The spires of the surrounding mountains cradled the lake, guarding it like a precious jewel.

The small motor of the *Escape* made a *hum hum* rhythm as the boat glided over the glassy surface past Starr Farm Beach, Mill's Point, Thayer Beach, and on into Malletts Bay. All boats had to be registered and in the bay by 5:30 a.m. to qualify. They arrived with minutes to spare.

In the shadow of the mountains, the heat came and went with the sun, and the sun would not rise for another hour. Kallie shivered, then tightened the straps on her neoprene life jacket. Reaching for the thermos of hot chocolate, she poured herself a steaming cup and let the sweet, dark liquid trickle down her throat and warm her insides.

Lake Champlain's Big Bass Bonanza was a Labor Day tradition. It was Grandpa Jess's favorite day of the year. The tournament ran from 7 a.m. until weigh-in at 3 p.m. There were prizes for both smallmouth and largemouth bass. Grandpa Jess claimed he didn't care much for the prizes—it was the thrill of the competition—though Kallie suspected he wasn't being entirely truthful.

He had taken part in the event since long before Kallie was born, winning one of the fifteen prizes each year. The only missing trophy on his shelf was the year Kallie's mother drowned. That year, the *Escape* had been stolen. It turned up days later, abandoned on the Canadian shore. Police said it had most likely been taken for a joyride by teenage delinquents. Since the boat hadn't been damaged, there was nothing more to be done about it.

"I can't," Kallie had said, shrinking at the mere thought. "Please don't ask me."

"But I need a twosome to form a team," Grandpa Jess had begged. "Or I'll be disqualified."

"Why can't you go, Dad?" She did her best to keep her tone in check, because she knew how much her father disliked the sound of whiny children.

Victor Jones shook his head briskly. "There's been a water main break on Pine Street. We've already received a flurry of calls about flooding damage and expect plenty more tomorrow. Customers are frantic. The adjusters are going mad—they all need my help. And Grandpa needs yours." He used the tone of voice he saved for speeches designed to instill responsibility. And guilt.

Grandpa Jess had looked at Kallie with large, pleading eyes.

"No," she had said definitively. "I can't."

The thought of being out on the lake—especially in the darkness, and on that particular weekend—made her stomach turn. Grandpa Jess meant the world to her, but not even for him could she force herself to do it. She never went out on the lake. Not ever.

"You have to get past this," said Grandpa Jess.

"You can't let fear control your life. The lake is not your enemy."

Kallie hung her head and closed her eyes. It was her enemy. Why couldn't he see that? It was deep and dark and mysterious, and it had stolen something from her. No. She would not go out on the lake. Not even for Grandpa Jess. But when she looked up to tell him so, she could taste his disappointment. She took a deep breath and sighed.

"I'm not fishing," she had said, as they set out from the marina.

"Leave that to me." Grandpa Jess grinned.

She adjusted the life jacket once again and hunkered into her seat. She finished the last few sips of hot chocolate and then sat yawning and staring out at the dark water.

"Keep your eyes open for ol' Champ." Grandpa chuckled.

Kallie scowled. She rubbed her eyes and stretched. There was a moment of long-drawn-out silence as the boat pulled into the bay, and then, as if the words came from a mouth other than hers, she heard herself ask, "Why were they going to Platts-burgh?"

Grandpa Jess was preparing the red anchor to moor the boat. He stopped and looked up. "What?"

"They were taking the ferry to Plattsburgh that day. What were they going to do there?"

"Uh, well." Grandpa Jess let the heavy red an-chor shaped like an upside-down mushroom splash over the side of the boat. It disappeared downward. "Business."

"What kind of business?" said Kallie. "I thought Dad did all his business in Burlington. And Mom stayed home. Writing."

"Personal business," he said. "Which means none of ours."

Personal. She mulled over the word. Personal meant private. Private meant secret. Then, like a weather vane catching a breeze, Kallie spun the con-versation in an entirely different direction.

"Did she love me?"

The anchor had reached the bottom. The boat was secure. Grandpa Jess stood staring over the side.

The full moon was large and looming. It reflected in the dark water and lit his face. He inched toward her and gently patted her knee.

"Of course she loved you." Though he tried to sound positive, there was something in his voice Kallie didn't like, something that said she was asking the wrong question. He patted her knee again and then began organizing his gear.

Kallie yawned deeply. They had to get up at three o'clock to get to the boat in order to reach the bay on time. She required exactly eight hours of sleep to function properly. She checked her watch. She was several hours short.

Grandpa Jess assembled his six-foot fishing rod and baited his hook. He pitched it into the lake about twenty feet from the boat. He liked to use a technique called flipping, where he pulled on the line, then let the weight of the lure sink it back down, pull the line up again—without using the reel—and let it sink again. He claimed it mesmerized the bass into biting.

Pull and sink. Pull and sink. Kallie watched him and waited. Waited and watched. Grandpa's dark silhouette bobbed and swayed in a hypnotizing rhythm while gentle waves flapped like crows' wings against the side of the boat. Kallie closed her eyes and let the boat rock her gently side to side.

Suddenly, she sensed movement, and her eyes snapped open. Grandpa Jess was tugging on the line. He pulled tighter and harder, and she knew he was in fight mode. He yanked and pulled, and the line grew taut, the tip of the rod bending with a heavy burden as he reeled in something huge.

"This is gonna be a big one!" he shouted. "Hold on, Kallie. Hold tight!"

Grandpa Jess braced himself against the side of the boat and began to crank the reel harder, pulling with such force Kallie thought the line would snap.

She leaned over to see what he'd caught. In the deep, velvety darkness, something emerged from the surface of the lake.

Kallie had expected the shimmering scales of a largemouth bass or a trout, but what appeared was pale with a bluish tinge. It took Kallie a moment to realize it was a human face.

The head emerged from the water with bluish skin, deep and cavernous eyes, and hair matted and

tangled with weeds. The black lips parted in a ghoulish grin while crablike limbs reached for her.

She recoiled, pressing herself into the side of the
boat and searching frantically for Grandpa Jess, but
he had vanished.

"Come," said the creature, crawling up over the
edge of the boat, grabbing hold of Kallie's arms. She
struggled wildly, kicking and scratching, but the thing
was cold and slimy and strong. She was overpowered,
and in one swift motion she was dragged overboard.

Icy water enveloped her and sucked her below its
inky depths. Her glasses were lost, and her life vest
came loose and drifted away. She tried to scream, but
as she opened her mouth, water rushed in, filling her
lungs with mud and minerals. Her chest seared. Her
struggling stalled. Her limbs began to wilt . . .

"I'm here, Kaliope . . ." she heard it say as darkness enveloped her. Smothered her. And then everything stopped.

Kallie startled awake. She spun around, her brain
still lost somewhere beneath the soupy surface of
sleep. She gasped for air. She was not underwater. She

was in the *Escape*. She was still wearing her life jacket. And her glasses. She was okay. She had dozed off.

The first glimmer of light crept over the horizon. Kallie squinted. In the mellow orange glow, Kallie saw Grandpa Jess holding his first bass.

"It's a lunker, Kallie!" He was grinning. "A lunker!"

Beside her, the thermos of hot chocolate had spilled. Kallie searched for a rag to clean the mess. She felt icy inside and out.

It was going to be a long day.

14

STILL LIFE

"Sincerely, Lucy."

Kallie lowered her assignment paper and looked up at the class with a smug, satisfied grin.

There was a moment of complete and utter silence, and then Pole began to slowly clap. Anna and Taylor joined in, creating what amounted to very sparse applause.

"Um. Thank you, Kallie," said Ms. Beausoleil, her face twisted into a mixture of confusion and shock. "That was very—" she seemed to search for the right word "—*informative*."

"I don't get it," said Ivan, shaking his head.

"Me either," said Mathusha.

"What about the wardrobe?" whispered Queenie. "She didn't even mention the wardrobe."

Kallie's letter from Lucy to her mother lasted twenty-five minutes and somehow included a lengthy discussion on the causes and consequences of World War II, the global conditions preceding World War I, fascism, racism, and concluded with an explanation of existentialism—the philosophical approach emphasizing the individual as a free person who determines his or her fate through acts of free will.

Rather pleased with herself, Kallie left the front of the class and plunked herself onto the giant, paisley pillow beside Pole, ignoring the dust cloud she'd created.

"Yes. Well. Perhaps next time, I should be a little more specific," muttered Ms. Beausoleil as she jotted notes into her assessment binder. She looked up, slightly frazzled, then tucked a curl behind her ear and said, "After Kallie's lecture . . . er, I mean, *letter*, we only have time for one more presentation. Anna, would you like to go?"

Anna beamed. She took the stage and read her letter softly.

Dearest Mother,

> *I have failed you. I am a traitor. Through my selfishness and greed, many have suffered, including those I love most. I betrayed Lucy, Susan, and Peter to the wicked White Witch. I lied to everyone, but most of all, I lied to myself. I convinced myself that the White Witch meant my sisters and brother no harm and that I was somehow deserving of the high honor she promised. You made great sacrifices to send us to safety, and now, because of me, everyone is in danger. But there is still hope. It lies in the real magic of the world. The magic to transform and redeem. I hope I shall redeem myself or die trying.*
>
> > *With much love and great hope,*
> >
> > > *your son,*
> > >
> > > *Edmund*

Anna looked up at the class as though searching for approval. The applause was soft but steady. Kallie noticed Ms. Beausoleil wiping something from the corner of her eye. Probably a speck of dust from the ratty old pillows.

They spent next period in science class. Mr. Bent had begun their first unit on the properties of matter. He explained how the density of a substance could be measured and quantified. Today, they were learning how to calculate the density of regular- and irregular-shaped objects. It was the only thing that got her through the morning, since the following period was nearly as bad as English.

Mr. Washington had positioned a large table in the center of the art room. On it, he placed several stacks of books and boxes to create levels. Over that, he draped a brown burlap cloth, and then, on each of the levels, he placed objects. A tin can filled with paintbrushes, a thick book with a pair of glasses on top, a vase containing three paper daisies, a candle-stick with a half-melted wax candle, a box of tissue, a coffee cup and a bag of cheese pretzels (Kallie suspected this was Mr. Washington's snack), and a small globe.

Chairs had been arranged in a circle around the

table. Once everyone was seated, he gave each student a large clipboard, a sheet of paper, and a piece of charcoal. Mr. Washington's instructions were simple—select an area of the still life table and sketch what you see. To keep students focused, he played classical music in the background. Kallie found the entire experience unnerving.

For the longest time, Kallie stared at the table festooned with objects. She had no clue as to where to begin. Mr. Washington made his rounds, complimenting each student on their work, assisting where necessary. When he arrived at Kallie, he placed a hand on her shoulders and whispered, "It's okay. There is no right or wrong here. Let your eyes guide your hands. Draw what you feel."

Kallie glanced at her empty paper and sighed. *I am drawing what I feel*, she thought.

She looked up again at the table and settled on the box of tissue. It was a simple rectangular prism. This was geometry. She could do this. Only, her eyes became distracted by the floppy white tissue hanging lazily out from the open slit. With only ten minutes left for the activity, she closed her eyes and began to scrape her charcoal across the paper. A line. Then another. And another. And suddenly, her hand was zipping up and down, side to side, pressing harder, then softer, swirling and curling. She had no idea what she was doing. But when she opened her eyes, a group of students had gathered around her.

"Wow," said Mathusha.

"That's great!" said Anna.

Pole was glaring at her suspiciously. "I had no idea you could draw like that."

Kallie was confused. She had never spent any time drawing. Her father didn't even allow coloring books. She had zero talent for art and couldn't understand what all the fuss was about. She looked down at what she'd done. As the sketch came into focus, her insides turned to jelly.

15

THE CASTLE

Liah tucked the bone flute into her sack. It was in its right-ful place once again. The Lie-peddler was gone, and along with him all evidence he had been there. He left no trace except for the melody he had played, for it still clung to the instrument, echoing on in her mind.

Liah had not slept well. The ground had been hard and pockmarked with pebbles, and the night too cold for comfort. She had drifted in and out of dreams. And now, as she gathered her belongings and prepared to set out, she found herself stifling yawns.

Facing the two paths, Liah could see one moved straight toward steep hills while the other meandered around the edge of the woods, meeting up once again with the river.

"Which road leads to the palace?"

"Both," said the bone carver. He slung his sack over his shoulder, adjusting its weight. "One is quicker, the other less perilous."

"Then which will we choose?"

He paused and stared out over the vast expanse he had traveled many times before. "It is never wise to trade time for security."

And with those words, he set out on the long and winding path. "Another half-day's journey and we will arrive at the base of the palace."

Liah refilled the gourds with water from the river. The meat supper had saved them two millet cakes. She supposed she should be grateful to the Lie-peddler for that, though something about the stranger continued to disturb her. She took a cake from her sack and broke it in two, offering the larger half to the bone carver. They chewed silently as they walked.

As they left the river, the dry fields of sorghum and millet eventually gave way to a rocky terrain. Once again, Liah's feet began to ache. She reached for her heel where a large blister had swollen.

The bone carver called out, "We have much distance to cover. You must not tarry."

"My skin is raw," Liah complained. "My feet ache terribly."

He stared at her a thoughtful moment and then said, "If something harms you, it is a sign that you must make a change."

"A change?" asked Liah. "But how, when I have no other shoes?"

The bone carver did not reply. He merely shrugged, turned, and slowly walked on.

"Make a change," Liah scoffed, rubbing her heel. "How can I make a change when I have but one pair of shoes?"

She took a ginger step, then another, the straw now cutting viciously into the blister, bursting it and exposing the fresh but vulnerable skin beneath. She stopped again and removed her shoe. The breeze was cool and stung, but at least the foot was free. Staring at it, she understood. She did not need another pair of shoes to make a change. She simply needed to remove those she wore and walk barefoot.

The bone carver let her travel this way for some time, and then, without glancing back, he tossed something over his shoulder. It landed in a small heap on the ground before her.

Liah bent to see what he had so casually cast aside and discovered it was a pair of goatskin shoes—his finest pair. Her immediate thought was that the bone carver must have pitched them accidentally. But when she caught up to him, holding the shoes out, he made no move to take them. He glanced at her, smiled, and then continued on his way.

Liah was filled with great joy and appreciation at the special gift. She pulled the shoes on, wriggling her toes in the supple leather. She was not sure if it was the softness of the shoes or the kind gesture of the bone carver that made the rest of the journey seem to pass all the quicker.

As they drew near the castle, more and more merchants joined their travels. They came from all directions, some on foot, others in ox-drawn carts. Liah made note of the many goods they bore: reams of fine silk, earthen jugs, animal pelts. Some carted bushels of fruit and vegetables, while others brought woven tapestries.

When at last Liah and the bone carver reached the base of a jagged mountain, the sun was only beginning to creep over the horizon. The orange dawn was fiercely bright, forcing Liah to squint and shade her eyes as she gazed upward.

Looming atop a rugged peak sat a daunting fortress that seemed to defy gravity. From its perch, the great palace cast a deep shadow far and wide.

Standing at the bottom, looking up, Liah got a sense of its impenetrability. The thick walls of stone surrounding the castle were high, and the twisting path leading up the cliff steep and narrow. Liah knew many enemy forces had tried unsuccessfully to breach the palace, but this was a castle devoted to one simple purpose—maintaining power.

The line of hopeful merchants was long and winding. It coiled its way toward the steep path leading upward.

"You will wait here," said the bone carver.

How badly Liah wished to pass through the wall to the great palace—to see the lavish displays of wealth and power with her own eyes. But all she could do was lower her head in acceptance. The bone carver left without looking back. He joined the lengthy line.

Liah plunked herself down on a nearby rock, retrieved one of the gourds from her sack, and took a sip of cold river water. If only there were a way she might take a quick peek—just a peek—and then return without her master's knowledge.

The sun rose higher in the sky. As Liah returned the

gourd to her sack, her hand grazed the damaged bone cup. She withdrew the piece and examined it. The scrapes were still visible, but only on one side. If she held it a certain way, the damage could be concealed. It was a very fine piece indeed. Much finer by far than her paltry carvings. Her bone flute paled in comparison.

Suddenly, the Lie-peddler's melody began worming its way through her mind once again. It brought with it an idea—a clever, but deceitful idea. There was a way she could glimpse the palace. If only for a moment. Using the cup, she could gain access and then return without the bone carver's knowledge.

Liah knew this was wrong. An unspoken truth was no better than a lie. She knew if she were caught, she would be severely punished. But the music whirled around and around in her head, entwining itself with her thoughts.

She was desperate to see the palace. Just one tiny glimpse. And perhaps it truly was no lie if the bone carver never knew to ask.

She sprung to her feet and scrambled to join the others. The path upward was treacherous, no more than three feet wide, steep and uneven. Her footing must be sure and solid, or she would plunge over the edge of the cliff.

Partway up, Liah began to notice strange wooden boxes clinging to the rocky flanks as though suspended by magic. The boxes were dark and rutted, and they appeared to have been carved from hollowed-out tree trunks. She had not noticed the boxes from the foot of the mountain, as the old wood blended into the shadows of the gray and brown stone. With each one she passed, she grew more curious as to what purpose they served—though, fearing her true motives might be discovered, she kept her head bent and spoke to no one.

At last, Liah reached the top of the mountain and stood before a great entrance guarded by a thousand armor-clad figures. Fabricating her lie, Liah approached the guards. She claimed her master had forgotten one of his precious carvings. Hiding the scuff, she held out the magnificent cup. Struck by its beauty and craftsmanship, the guard let her pass.

Once through the enormous wall, Liah followed the other merchants into the palace. As she passed through the great wooden doors, she gazed about, her jaw slackening with amazement. Enormous alabaster columns sprung from gleaming marble floors stretching toward a high gilded ceiling encrusted with sparkling jewels.

The walls were adorned with enormous, embroidered tapestries, thick and lush, and each telling a tale. At either end of the room, grand staircases curled upward, their railings fashioned from giant pearls and sea coral. Liah's eyes strained to take in all the grandeur and opulence of the space as she made her way toward an archway that led out to a courtyard nearly as large as Liah's entire village. Once outside, she slipped away from the crowd and ducked into the shadows.

Strange animals of all sizes moved freely through the space—horned beasts, spotted beasts, and countless exotic birds. There were all sorts of trees and potted plants. And in the center of the courtyard was a great scarlet pond—the one she'd heard tell of. By its earthy, acrid aroma, Liah recognized immediately it was not filled with blood, but rather with wine.

Drunken guests lazed about, dipping cups, allowing the fermented, tannic liquid to spill down their chins and stain their garbs, while others drifted in small boats, plucking skewers of roasted bird—quail, thought Liah—suspended from a large tree on an island in the center of the pool.

And high above the courtyard, on a stone belvedere,

surveying the chaos beneath her, sat the Empress. From the distance, she appeared thin and statuesque, swathed in fine cloth of flax thread and spun gold.

Liah was somewhat disappointed, for none of the whisperings had been true. There was no blood pond, no forest of roasted enemies, and the Empress appeared no larger than herself. Not at all the imposing figure Liah had come to expect.

So mesmerized by all the detail was she, Liah nearly missed the small figure of the bone carver. He stood in line, awaiting his audience with the Empress. As though sensing her presence, he turned sharply toward her.

16

THE POWER OF SUGGESTION

The charcoal slipped from Kallie's fingers. It dropped to the floor along with the clipboard that landed at her feet with a hollow *thud*.

Kallie stood, her knees trembling. "Not feeling well," she muttered, sweeping past Mr. Washington, who had stooped to pick up her drawing.

She left the class as quickly as she could without breaking her stride. She marched down the corridor and burst through the door to the girl's washroom. Fortunately, it was empty.

Something was happening to her. Something completely and totally beyond her control. It was as if she had become a puppet and someone was working the strings.

It was a terrifying feeling not knowing what might happen next. But something was coming. She could feel it, but she could not yet see it. She did not even know where to look.

She reached out a shaky hand and turned on the faucet. She scooped cold water, splashed her face, and then took several cleansing breaths. She stared hard at her piqued complexion in the small mirror hanging above the sink. At long last she regained some composure. Rule number one in any crisis: Remain calm.

The fourth piece from the box had a castle on it. And now, on the art paper, etched in dark, bold lines, shaded perfectly, was a castle. It sat perched high on a cliff, with a narrow road winding up toward its entrance. At the base of the mountain stood a small, cloaked figure. In one of the castle windows was a blurry face, staring down, ghostly.

She'd sketched all of it. A perfect castle with shadows and highlights, value and texture. There was depth and contrast and even a hint of movement. And she'd done it all without even looking at the paper.

Kallie shook her head as though responding to an

invisible inquisitor. No. She could not have been the artist. There was no way. She had zero talent. She was certain of it. She'd *made* certain of it. *Hadn't she?*

A short time later, Pole and Anna approached Kallie, who sat despondent at what had somehow become their usual lunch table. She was staring sullenly at the triangular tuna and alfalfa half-sandwich in her hand.

When she saw them, she frowned. They were walking side by side. Close together. As though they were friends. Best friends.

"Mr. Bent likes the idea, but he feels we need support from the student body before going to Principal McEwan," Pole was saying.

"We can make flyers!" beamed Anna. "And get signatures. And I was thinking we could have a Periodic Picnic Table Lunch, an Element Dash, a Guess the Element contest . . ."

"Great idea about the flyers," said Pole. "I'll work on it tonight. And by the way, I've decided I'm going to be helium."

"You would choose a gas," giggled Anna.

Kallie frowned harder.

"What's wrong?" asked Pole, seating himself across from Kallie. "Why did you run out of art class?"

"You left your binder," said Anna, placing it on the table. She took a sip of water from her cup.

Kallie eyed the jagged line of glue where it had been repaired. She opened her lunch bag and retrieved a second container. She handed it to Anna.

"What's this?"

"I know you eat huge breakfasts," said Kallie. "But I made an extra sandwich. For you. Just in case . . ."

Anna took the container and smiled. "Yes. Mrs. Winslow really outdid herself again this morning. I am pretty stuffed"—she patted her belly—"but maybe just a bite . . ."

Pole stared at Kallie as though she had grown a second head. She was not acting like herself. And she hadn't answered his questions. Mostly because she wasn't sure what she could tell him.

He opened his lunch bag and unwrapped a tofu burrito. "What's happened to you? You're acting irrationally."

Kallie's eyes shot daggers in his direction. It was the worst thing he had ever said to her. First, he shows up with Anna as if they've been best friends forever, planning Periodic Table Day without her, and now he insults her. He was right, of course, but that did nothing to dull the sting. She knew she wasn't acting sensibly. But couldn't he see it wasn't her fault? Something was recklessly guiding her actions. He'd know that—if he weren't paying so much attention to his new friend.

Kallie swallowed a bite of sandwich and secretly scolded herself. Emotions were untrustworthy, and hers were running amok. She took a deep breath and reminded herself that truly smart people know they do not know everything. A truly smart person knows when it's time to seek help. And if anyone could help her, surely it was Pole.

"Can I tell you something?" she said. "Will you listen to the whole story before you pass judgment?"

"A story!" said Anna. "Hurray! Does it have fairies? And trolls? Because those are my favorites! Or is it more of a mystery? Oh! A romance! Oh, please say it's a romance!" She clapped her hands vigorously.

A sinking feeling settled into Kallie's stomach. She put down her sandwich. Things were much worse than she had thought. She was no longer in control of her actions or her words.

"It's not a *story*." She corrected herself. "It's merely a . . . a . . . recounting of events . . . of happenings . . . of occurrences. A report. Yes. That's what I meant to say. A report."

Anna looked deflated and slightly peevish.

"Something is happening to me," Kallie said softly.

She watched Pole intently, his face as unreadable as a book of squiggles and squares. But he was a good listener. Kallie knew he approached everything scientifically, so she was certain he'd gather all the facts and hear everything she had to say before forming an opinion.

Slowly, methodically, Kallie recounted the events leading up to the drawing, including the faceless man, the box, the nine pieces, and their connection to recent events in her life: the jackal. The broken cup. The ocarina. And now the castle.

Anna sprung to her feet, a wild glint in her eyes.

She pointed an *aha* finger in the air. "I know exactly what those things are! The pieces—inside the box—they're story bones!"

"What?" said Kallie.

"You know—story bones!" she repeated excitedly.

Kallie and Pole shook their heads, looking blank.

"You've never heard of story bones?" said Anna incredulously. She looked in disbelief from Kallie to Pole, but both shrugged.

"It's like a game. You toss the bones," said Anna, "then use the pictures to create a story. Only, yours are bewitched, don't you see? And now you've become part of the story!" Her triumphant gaze swung like a pendulum from one lackluster expression to the other.

Pole averted his eyes and cleared his throat. "Well. That certainly could be one explanation. But I offer another, slightly more plausible one. What I think you have here, Kallie, is a simple case of the *power of suggestion*."

His eyes were steadfast, his voice calm, bordering on casual, which put Kallie immediately at ease.

"The idea a person—or object—can guide the

thoughts, feelings, and even behavior of another. Influence their surroundings. It's nothing new. Simple nineteenth-century psychology." He tucked a straying piece of lettuce into his burrito.

"The power of suggestion," Kallie repeated slowly, with each word becoming all the more convinced.

Anna frowned and shook her head defiantly.

"Consider it, Anna," said Pole. "If something has been planted in our mind, and we come to expect a certain outcome, then we automatically set in motion a chain of thoughts and behaviors producing that exact outcome."

Anna narrowed her eyes. "I still say the pieces are story bones . . . bewitched story bones . . ."

"You're right as usual, Pole," said Kallie. "I saw the pictures on the pieces from the box. I must have stored the images in my subconscious and then went about re-creating them in my life . . . Or something like that, anyway."

Pole took a huge bite of his burrito. "Precisely." A black bean fell out of his mouth and onto the table.

"The power of suggestion," repeated Kallie. "That has to be it."

"Of course it is." He popped the bean into his mouth. "So stop thinking about that box. Clear your head. Put it away. Out of sight. Out of mind."

Kallie nodded. Clear her head. That was the solution. The box had caused the exact trouble her father had warned her about. It had fueled her unconscious mind and let it run wild. He'd be furious with her if he found out. It was time to rid herself of the box and regain control of herself and her surroundings.

"Out of curiosity," said Anna, finishing the last bite of her sandwich. She sealed the container and handed it back to Kallie. "What were the next pictures on those cubes?"

"Well," said Kallie. "There was a cylinder spouting flames, and then a coffin, and then . . ."

"A coffin?" gasped Anna. "Oh no. That can't be good. Luckily you're putting a stop to this suggestion power straightaway. Before things get really bad."

"Yeah." Kallie gulped. "Good thing."

17

THE UNSINKABLE TRUTH

The rest of the day sailed on like a seven-masted schooner. Kallie knew she could count on Pole to be the voice of reason. She dismissed all the strange happenings as mere coincidence—what else could they be?—and did her best to put them and the box out of her head.

Still, Anna had sown a tiny seed of doubt, which already began to take root. On the very odd and unlikely chance Anna was right, something terrible was going to happen, and Kallie had no way of knowing what it would be, let alone how to prevent it.

That afternoon was gym class. Physical education was the least offensive of all the nonacademic subjects as Kallie recognized the body's need for daily, vigorous activity. She owned a well-worn copy of *Brain Training: Physical Exercises to Enhance Academic Achievement*. She lifted one arm and circled the other while performing deep lunges.

"Bench!" called Coach Mandala.

Kallie frowned and took her seat. She continued drawing giant infinity symbols in the air, known as *lazy eights*. Next she began yawning while massaging her cheeks. "Energy yawns," she said to Anna. "Provides oxygen to the brain while relaxing the eyes. Helps promote motor control."

Anna joined her.

As Kallie waited for her turn to sub into the flag football game, her eyes wandered to Anna's shorts—the same ones she'd sported the first day they'd seen each other in the marketplace. Anna followed Kallie's gaze and then ran her hands over them, concealing spots where the threads had worn thin.

"I have a trunkful of designer clothes at home.

Really expensive stuff," said Anna, "but Mrs. Winslow doesn't like me dressing too fancy. She's worried someone might get the idea I'm extremely wealthy and try to abduct me. She's such a worrywart."

"I like that shade of yellow," said Pole. "It reminds me of my mother's homemade lemon curd." He grinned.

Kallie rolled her eyes. "How long do you have to live with Mrs. Winslow?"

"Well," said Anna thoughtfully. "I told you my parents were magicians, right?"

"The Amazing Alonzo and his Alluring Assistant Ava," said Kallie, recalling the previous conversation.

"Well, then," she sighed. "I suppose it's time I tell you the whole truth . . ."

"Jones! Glud! Offense!" shouted Coach Mandala. "Rodriguez—Defense!"

Kallie and Anna took to the field, but since neither could catch or throw, they hung as close to the sidelines as possible without stepping out of bounds, so as to avoid any unnecessary contact with the football. Pole was on the opposing team and stood facing them.

"You see," said Anna. "My father is a marvelous magician. He can do all sorts of amazing illusions. But he is most famous for his magic cabinet—an enormous, elaborately carved wooden box. He can make people and objects disappear."

Another box. One that makes people disappear. Kallie was sorry she'd asked.

"Well, he'd inherited the magic cabinet from another old magician he'd met in a pub one dark and stormy night. That magician had inherited it from another, who had inherited it from another, who . . ."

"Yes, yes," said Kallie. "We get the idea. Go on."

All eleven players were on the line of scrimmage preparing to run downfield, but Anna kept talking. She was able to talk at such a high speed she could get a thousand words out in an instant.

"The old magician said the cabinet possessed powerful magic—but you could use it only once each night. He warned my father never to do the trick more than once. Not ever, or . . ."

"Jones! Glud!" shouted Coach. "We're playing football here! Not having afternoon tea! Rodriguez— stay focused!"

Kallie glanced along the line at Ivan. He was the quarterback and was shouting numbers. The football was snapped, and everyone began to run downfield, except the three who strolled along in no particular hurry.

"Anyway, this one night . . ." Anna's voice dropped low. ". . . After my father had made my mother disappear and reappear, he was offered a great sum of money by a mysterious stranger in the audience to repeat the trick. It was so much money, my father couldn't say no."

"Touchdown!" shouted Jonah. He was doing a ridiculous dance in the end zone. Kallie thought it made him look like a cross between an amorous gorilla and an agitated chicken. Coach Mandala barked several instructions, and the players began to reorganize.

"So," said Anna. "Reluctantly, my mother stepped into the box a second time and disappeared. Except when it was time for her to return, the box remained empty."

"Wasn't she behind the stage?" asked Pole. "I know that trick. It works with trapdoors or mirrors."

Anna shook her head. "I told you, the box was real. It was magic. But it was cursed. My father had ignored the warning by doing the trick a second time, and so my mother was gone. My father spent all night trying to get her back, and when nothing worked, he stepped into the box himself to try to find her and bring her back, but then he disappeared, too. I'm staying with Mrs. Winslow until they return." Anna smiled. "Which should be any day now."

The ball flew so quickly across the field Kallie didn't have a chance to warn Pole. It hit him in the stomach, knocking him to the ground.

"Wake up, Rodriguez!" shouted Coach Mandala. "This isn't a slumber party!"

Kallie and Anna helped Pole to his feet. The wind had been knocked out of him. They stopped talking, keeping their eyes open for more assaulting footballs, but Kallie couldn't help but think about what Anna had told her.

After school, Kallie and Grandpa took their usual walk down the steep sidewalk toward the lake. As Pole suggested, she put the box so far out of her mind it was as if it had never existed. She felt almost lighter as they made their way back home—though she did notice Grandpa Jess was walking a bit slower and puffing a bit more than usual.

"Are you okay?" she asked.

"Never felt better," he said.

Grandpa Jess was a poor liar. She linked arms with him. They made it back up the incline together.

Kallie's father came home at his usual time. He washed up, and they all sat down to dinner. Grandpa Jess made sugar shack crêpes with ham and eggs and plenty of maple syrup. It was like breakfast, dinner, and dessert all in one. Kallie complained it was unhealthy as she passed Grandpa Jess her plate for a second helping.

"You need to start learning the family recipes," he said. "Or when I'm gone, they'll be lost."

Kallie's stomach jerked. "Don't talk like that, Grandpa."

"Oh, pay him no mind," said her father. "Grandpa Jess is as strong as an ox. He'll outlast us all."

"This was one of your mother's favorite meals," said Grandpa.

Kallie's eyes darted toward her father. She held his gaze a moment, trying to discern his thoughts, but his expression was unreadable.

"That was delicious," he said. "I'm stuffed." He lifted his plate and took it to the sink, where he began to clean up.

After dinner, Kallie and her father played a few games of chess. He adored strategy games like chess, Go, Nine Men's Morris, and Mancala. He'd taught her these at a very young age and praised her often, claiming she had developed into quite a worthy opponent.

Content with having won once, Kallie went up to her room and got ready for bed. She was about to doze off when she overheard her grandfather and father talking in the kitchen. At first, they spoke in hushed voices, which grew increasingly louder.

"You can't get away with this forever," said Grandpa. "One day the truth will come out . . . and then you'll have to pay for what you've done . . ."

"That day isn't today," said her father. "You'd do best to let sunken ships stay sunk."

"Ah, but the truth always rises to the surface. The truth is unsinkable."

"Yes, well, they said that about the *Titanic*, didn't they? And where is it now?"

18

PARTNERS IN CRIME

The next few days passed without disruption or peculiar happenings. The dull routine brought back Kallie's sense of focus and purpose. Unfortunately, it also lulled her into a false sense of security.

At least she had avoided reading for Ms. Beausoleil. She had had a series of unfortunate—yet timely—ailments, including a dry throat, a wiggly tooth, cracked lips, blurred vision caused by an allergic reaction to the dust mites in the pillows . . . She had even gone so far as to try to form a society for non-read-alouds—known as the NRABC—Non-Read-Aloud by Choice—but no one except Pole had joined, and so they were forced to disband.

"*And that is the very end of the adventures of the wardrobe*," read Anna.

Kallie sighed. "Thank goodness for that."

"*But . . .*"

"I knew it," snapped Pole. "Never let your guard down."

"*. . . if the Professor was right it was only the beginning of the adventures of Narnia.*"

"The beginning! How can it be the beginning?" said Kallie.

"There's always a catch to these fantasies." Pole scoffed. "They never let you just move on peacefully." He punched his pillow. A cloud of dust enveloped him. He coughed, fanning the air.

"Yes, well, now I suppose I'll just have to read the others in the series," grumbled Kallie vaguely. Pole shot her a look with a raised eyebrow. "For closure," she added hastily.

Ms. Beausoleil took the book from Anna and sighed dreamily. A lengthy discussion of theme, motif, character, and arcs ensued. And just when Kallie thought the worst of it was over, the teacher cleared her throat.

"And now, for your next assignment . . ."

Kallie braced herself. How bad could it be? It couldn't be worse than the letter. Could it?

". . . a diorama depicting one of the settings in the novel . . ."

There was a flurry of questions and comments.

"Can we pick any setting?" asked Mathusha.

"I just threw out a shoebox," Taylor said with a sigh.

"Can I use a 3-D printer?" asked Pole.

To add insult to injury, Ms. Beausoleil added, "And you'll be working with a partner."

There was a moment of voiceless frenzy. Eyes darted round the room. Secret pacts were made with simple nods, waves, and pointing. Kallie didn't have to resort to any such insecurities. Everyone knew she and Pole would be partners. As always.

Regrettably, Ms. Beausoleil had other plans.

"I'll be assigning the pairs," she said cheerfully.

The dissolution of the previously made pacts was not nearly as silent as their making. Ms. Beausoleil waved off the protests and began forming groups.

"Jonah and Queenie . . . Grace and Ivan . . . Taylor and Mathusha . . ."

No one said a word, but smiles fell and eyes rolled.

". . . Pole and Saif . . ."

Pole glanced at Kallie and shrugged apologetically even though it had been completely out of his control.

". . . Kallie and . . ."

Kallie held her breath.

". . . Anna."

Anna's smile was so large it nearly wrapped around her head. Kallie returned it with a half-hearted wave and a grin one might easily confuse with a painful grimace.

"Well. I suppose we should meet tomorrow, seeing as it's Saturday, to get a head start," Kallie said. They had been given the last five minutes of class to organize themselves. "I have allotted myself some *free time* in my schedule. I can come to your place . . . I mean, Mrs. Winslow's . . ."

"Sure. Of course. We could do that. That would be great," Anna said. "But, well, Mrs. Winslow is a bit eccentric. She's absolutely paranoid about having strangers in her house, what with it being so huge and posh and what with her having all that expensive china and valuable crystal and . . ."

Kallie frowned. "You make it sound like I'd break something."

"No. No. It's not you," said Anna reassuringly. "It's Mrs. Winslow. She's odd like that. How about I come to your place? We'll need paint, of course, and construction paper, and . . ."

"Whoa." Kallie waved her hands in front of her face. "I don't have any *crafty* things." She said it as though it were something distasteful bordering on illegal.

"All right. Then we'll have to buy some," said Anna resolutely. "There's a variety shop on Willard Street. Maybe we can get some stuff there."

"Maybe . . ." said Kallie. Then she had another thought. "Or how about the Dollar Basket just past the interstate? Where did you say you lived?"

Anna looked side to side. "I'm really not supposed to say . . ."

"For heaven's sake," said Kallie. "Do I look like a

thief or an ax murderer? Just tell me where you live so we can coordinate."

Anna paused for a brief moment. "South Prospect," she said quietly. "Near the campus."

Kallie knew the area. It had enormous brick homes with timbered gables, castlelike turrets, and ancient trees on huge properties. Many had been transformed into fraternity and sorority houses over the years. Those that hadn't had been in families for generations—people with what Grandpa called *old money.*

"Perfect," said Kallie. "I'll ride my bike up Ledge Road and meet you. Do you have a bike?"

"Oh, Mrs. Winslow has several. It's only a matter of selecting the color and style. But I'll need to meet you there. I have a few things to do in the morning, so I'm not exactly sure where I'll be."

Kallie agreed, and all was settled. "We'll get everything we need at the shop."

"And I'm sure Mrs. Winslow won't mind if I use one of her shoeboxes—she literally has dozens. That way we'll be all set for Monday. We're going to make the best partners!"

The following morning, Kallie awoke at her usual time. She got dressed, had breakfast, and prepared for her journey. She picked up the old photograph, studied it intently, then placed it back on the shelf.

"I'm in sixth grade now," she said, slinging a small brown purse over her shoulder. "I can go on my own."

Grandpa Jess stroked his beard. "I'm not sure . . ."

"Dad said I could when I asked him this morning. He said I would *benefit greatly from added responsibility.*"

"Well," said Grandpa, not sounding all too convinced. "If you're sure."

"Positive," said Kallie. Her brown eyes were steady and resolute.

Kallie reached into the hall closet and grabbed her maroon cable-knit cardigan. She didn't like that it had mismatching gold buttons, but Grandpa had given it to her. Apparently, Grandma Gem had been an excellent knitter. This was the only piece Kallie had inherited from her. It was a bit large, but cozy, and perfect for days you just wanted to wrap yourself in a blanket.

"What's the name of the store?" asked Grandpa Jess. "Where's it located?"

"The Dollar Basket," said Kallie. "On Dorset, near highway two."

"Oh," said Grandpa Jess softly. "Are you sure you want to head all the way over there? You could try the variety shop just up the street."

"I don't think they'll have all the things we need," said Kallie. "Plus, the dollar store might be cheaper."

Grandpa Jess had a bit of a distant look in his eyes as he ran a hand down the sleeve of the old sweater. He made her promise to ride carefully.

It wasn't quite fall, but the air was crisp and smelled of woodstoves and fallen leaves. Kallie headed round the side of the house toward the garage and yanked open the old door. She was immediately smacked with a musty odor. The space was small and crammed with generations of Grandpa Jess's fishing gear. Tackle boxes, rubber boots, rods, reels, and other paraphernalia littered the tight space.

Carefully, she extracted her bike from behind a wall of junk. It was coated in dust. It reminded her of the bike on display at the aquarium—the one that had been submerged in the lake and was now covered with invasive zebra mussels.

She hadn't ridden it in ages. Luckily, it was still in fine working condition. She swung a leg over the bar, steadied herself, and began shakily pedaling, the handlebars teetering and wobbling until she gained control.

Kallie made her way along the breezy side streets. She'd calculated how long the ride would take so as to be sure she'd arrive on time. She'd made arrangements to meet Anna at precisely ten thirty. Only, when Kallie arrived, Anna wasn't there.

She rested her bike against the side of the building and paced in front of the store, staring at the basket on the sign made of dollar symbols. This was definitely the backdrop of the photograph on her shelf. She took a deep breath, unsure as to why she'd come and what she'd hoped to find.

All the while, she kept checking her watch. At two

minutes, she was annoyed. By five, she began to huff. And after ten minutes, she was positively beastly.

She entered the shop without Anna. She stomped up and down the aisles locating the craft section, glaring at all the paint and paste. She lifted a dusty tub of neon green and held it as though it contained radioactive waste.

"The trouble with being punctual is that nobody's there to appreciate it." She quoted Philadelphia reporter Franklin P. Jones.

"Is there something I can help you with?" said a kindly voice.

Kallie turned to see a robust middle-aged woman wearing a long denim skirt and purple Crocs. Over that, she wore an apron with the basket logo.

Kallie adjusted her glasses. "I'm waiting for someone." She didn't mean to sound quite so sharp, but her surprise at seeing the apron mingled with her anger at Anna's tardiness and spilled into her tone.

The woman smiled. "I know that sweater. How could I forget those mismatched gold buttons." She pointed to the top one with an anchor embossed on it.

Kallie pulled the wool cardigan tighter around

her waist. "My grandmother made it. Maybe she purchased the yarn here?"

The woman studied Kallie as though she were a speck on the horizon growing larger and clearer until finally a full picture was formed. The smile slipped from her lips, and she shook her head. "No. I don't think so," she said quietly.

The store clerk's demeanor had changed so suddenly Kallie thought it was very strange. She was about to question the woman further when Anna burst between them.

"Sorry I'm late! I told Mrs. Winslow I had to meet you at ten thirty, but she insisted that we head out early in the morning since it was the best time of year to pick blackberries and fresh kale, and she didn't want to miss out, and I said I'd only be a minute then hurry straight back home—"

Kallie wasn't listening. "It's fine," she said, cutting Anna's lengthy excuse short. "Let's just get the stuff we need. Grandpa Jess will worry if I'm late."

"Let me know if you need any help," said the clerk. The smile had returned to her face. She disappeared around the corner.

After some heated debate, Kallie and Anna agreed to construct Mr. Tumnus's cave. Kallie would make the *cave* part, and Anna would do the rest. They located several things they could use, including Styrofoam, felt, Plasticine clay, spools, and colored paper.

"Oh, gosh," said Anna, when they reached the checkout. "This is so embarrassing, but Mrs. Winslow had me in such a rush I forgot to bring money." She placed the items she carried on the conveyor belt.

Kallie sighed. She got out her wallet, paid, and handed Anna the bag. She didn't want to bring the bag of arts and crafts supplies home. It would invite too many unwanted questions. "Just don't *forget* to bring it all on Monday."

Kallie took one last look around the shop. The clerk Kallie had spoken to busied herself by rearranging the already neat rows of ribbon in front of the checkout. Kallie stood staring at her a moment longer, then finally turned to leave.

"Did you forget something?" said the woman.

Kallie spun round. "Pardon me?"

"The spools," she said, handing Kallie the small package. "You left them behind."

Kallie took it mechanically, pausing again, grappling for the right words. But when she opened her mouth, all she could muster was a brittle *thank you*.

Anna was already pedaling quickly down the street. Kallie hopped on her bike and scrambled to catch up to give Anna the spools. Kallie pumped her legs as hard as she could, but Anna was quicker and Kallie got stuck at a traffic light.

She thought for sure she'd catch Anna before she turned onto South Prospect—but when Anna arrived at that intersection, she went straight through it and then turned in the opposite direction once she reached Willard.

Odd, thought Kallie. Anna had said she had to return straight home to Mrs. Winslow. Kallie couldn't help but be curious. She continued to follow.

Though Kallie rode as quickly as she could, she was not used to such physical exertion, and she began to slow. From Willard, Anna turned onto North Street. Kallie nearly thought she'd lost her but then caught sight of the bike as it turned again onto one of the side streets.

Kallie stopped sharply when she saw Anna

dismount in front of a tiny, old house that had been extended backward into a townhouse complex. Anna leaned the bike she had been riding against the garage and then climbed the steps to what appeared to be a tiny apartment above.

Kallie wondered whom Anna could possibly be visiting. She thought perhaps she should go up to the door, knock on it, and see for herself. She gripped the package of spools tightly in her hand. Suddenly, giving them to Anna didn't seem so important, and an odd feeling came over Kallie, as though she were an intruder—exactly the kind of person Mrs. Winslow had warned Anna about.

Kallie put a foot to a pedal, turned her bike, and rode home.

———————— ·•· ————————

Grandpa Jess stood on the porch pacing. Kallie figured he'd probably been there the entire time worrying. He smiled when he saw her and ushered her into the kitchen, where he had a steaming bowl of chowder waiting.

"Did you find everything you need?" he asked.

Kallie nodded. She lifted a spoonful of thick soup and then set it back down. "Did the sweater belong to Grandma?"

Grandpa Jess coughed a few times and then took a sip of water. "Grandma Gem made it. I told you that when I gave it to you."

"Yes," said Kallie, eyeing him. "You said Grandma made it. But was it hers?"

Grandpa Jess lowered his eyes. "Finish your chowder, Kallie. Before it gets cold."

He left the kitchen abruptly. Kallie gathered the sweater in her arms. She breathed in deeply. She had never paid attention to its comforting scent. Lavender. With a hint of lily.

—— ·•· ——

First period Monday morning was science class. Mr. Bent was conducting an experiment on expansion and contraction, and Kallie was particularly proud when he selected her to be his assistant.

"Matter is not solid," said Mr. Bent. "In fact, it's

made of atoms and empty space. If we adjust that empty space, we can make solid matter grow or shrink. Let us demonstrate."

Kallie beamed as she put on a lab coat. There was no need for Mr. Bent to make sure her hair was out of the way, because it was already tied back in her usual tight ponytail.

Unfortunately, the safety goggles didn't fit over her prescription eyewear, so she had to remove them. Behind the scuffed plastic, her vision was fuzzy.

Mr. Bent asked Kallie to hold up two metal rods. On the end of one was a brass loop. On the other, a ball. He asked her to demonstrate how easily the brass ball could pass through the loop. She did so several times.

"Now," he said, "we will demonstrate how heat alters the particles, expanding the metal. Size, my friends, is merely an illusion."

Mr. Bent prepared the equipment. First, he checked the plastic tubing of the Bunsen burner thoroughly for any leaks. Next, he placed the burner on a heatproof mat, attached the tubing to the gas nozzle, and held a lit match to the top of the cylinder while slowly turning on the gas to light the flame. Finally, he prepared a beaker with cold water.

"Place the metal ball into the flame," instructed Mr. Bent.

Kallie held the rod over the flame as though she were lighting the Olympic torch.

"Now, try to pass it through the ring," he said.

Kallie stepped out from behind the counter so the class could get a clear view. She attempted to pass the ball through the same loop, but it wouldn't fit.

There were *oohs* and *ahhs*, and general murmuring, but just as Kallie was about to turn, Anna sprung to her feet.

"The flaming cylinder!" she shouted.

Kallie startled. She dropped the rod. Flustered and embarrassed, she scrambled to retrieve it. Without her glasses, she grabbed the wrong end. A searing pain lit her right hand. The rod clattered to the floor a second time.

— 19 —

THE FLAMING CYLINDER

Liah leaped behind a gathering of trees and shrubs, hiding herself among the large foliage. She pressed her back against the trunk of a tree and held her breath, hoping she had not been discovered.

"Great and powerful Empress . . ."

Liah heard a familiar voice. She peeked out from behind the shrubs. The bone carver was no longer gazing in her direction. He must not have seen her. She breathed a soft sigh of relief. She had been foolish to sneak into the palace. Her toes wriggled in the goatskin shoes, filling her with shame. She would wait until he was well distracted and slip out unnoticed. On their travels home, she would find the right moment to confess.

"Wise beyond years . . . whose cruelty is justified . . .

whose benevolence and grace know no bounds . . . feared by many . . . adored by all . . ."

It was the Lie-peddler who spoke. Liah had not seen him in the lengthy line. He had appeared as if out of nowhere, striding past the others straight to the front of the line. He stood below the terrace, gazing up at the Empress.

"What is it you come to sell?" she asked in a delicate, yet rigid voice.

The Lie-peddler folded his hands, raised them over his head, and bowed low in customary reverence. Then, Liah watched as he tilted his face upward, one sharp eye meeting the Empress's. "Lies."

Liah stifled a giggle. But if the Empress perceived the slight, she gave no indication. Instead, she remained still, reminding Liah of a cat, waiting for the right time to pounce upon its prey.

"I have no use for lies," she said, each word dripping from her lips like poisonous honey.

The Lie-peddler raised himself to his full height and grinned. "Of course not. How foolish of me. I forget you already have an elaborate selection of your own."

The Empress sat stiffly, her features frozen in a look of icy amusement. "You are familiar to me. You resemble an arrogant sot I had punished some time ago for displeasing me with his nonsense." She seemed to be thinking back fondly. "You could not be him, though, for his bones lie rotting unremembered and unattended."

"An interesting story," said the Lie-peddler. "Perhaps I might tell you one of my own? It is quite a remarkable tale. It tells of a great and terrible Empress who is vanquished with the bones of an old storyteller . . . and a little bit of magic."

Two guards stepped forward, but a slight wave of the Empress's hand stayed their swords.

"That may be interesting indeed," she said, calmly, "but I have a better one. Shall I tell you the tale of the storyteller who danced to his death?"

Her thin lips furled into a smile as a group of guards brought forth an enormous bronze cylinder. It was over twenty feet long and eight feet wide with wheels on each end that allowed it to rotate. They placed the cylinder over a bed of coals, lathered it in oil, and forced the Lie-peddler to walk on top. One of the guards lit the coals while others used fans to stoke the flames. As the cylinder grew hotter, the Lie-peddler shifted his feet to avoid burning.

Though the masses of drunken guests laughed and

jeered, the Lie-peddler remained staunch and fearless, with a determined, haughty look in his eyes as though he knew something none other did.

When at last the Lie-peddler slipped off the cylinder and into the fiery coals, the bone carver dropped his sack and sprang forth. Before the guards were any wiser, the bone carver had dragged the Lie-peddler out of the flames.

Liah watched in horror as a guard lay hold of the bone carver and thrust him before the Empress. But he rose tall and addressed her in an angered voice such that Liah had never heard.

"Your cruelty and corruption dishonor your ancestors. You neglect your people. You show no mercy. You rule with tyranny and malice. Renounce yourself, for you have lost all moral right to rule. Renounce yourself or your own people shall rise up against you, and your name shall echo with hatred for a thousand years."

The Empress's expression contorted into a foxlike grin. "Not only will you dance for me alongside this fool—but for your insolence your bones shall hang on my mountainside for a thousand years, as a warning to all who oppose or offend me."

The breath caught in Liah's throat—the boxes she'd

seen—they held bones. *Without proper bone burial, the spirit could never rest. It would wander the earth for all eternity.* She watched as the bone carver was thrown onto the cylinder along with the Lie-peddler. Both did their best to remain upright, but the metal glowed fiery red.

Liah could feel the unbearable heat from where she stood. Her heart fluttered inside her chest as she pressed her mind to think of a way to stop the madness. But what might she do? How could she fight a great army on her own? It would require strength, or magic, or both.

With tears streaming down her cheeks, she peered out from the shadows. The Lie-peddler caught her gaze. A deep sound rumbled inside his belly and burst forth from his mouth as he began to laugh.

"You are a greater fool than I thought," said the Empress, "for you laugh at your own demise."

"I laugh not at my demise," said the man, his face as flush as the fiery coals. "I laugh at yours. For even the strongest guards cannot protect one who has allowed her own doom to pass freely through her gates."

20

PERSONAL. PRIVATE. SECRET.

Kallie's pride hurt worse than her hand.

She tried to cover the red spot where a giant blister was forming. She insisted she was perfectly fine, but Mr. Bent sent her to the office for treatment all the same. The head secretary, Mrs. Hewlett, had a quick look at Kallie's hand.

"It doesn't appear too bad," she said, patting Kallie's head as though she were in preschool. "Have a seat in the health room. We'll get a cool compress on it. You can rest for a while, and we'll see if the swelling goes down."

"But I'm fine. I don't want to stay," protested Kallie, adjusting her glasses and smoothing her hair. "I'm missing science class."

"No buts."

Mrs. Hewlett ushered her into a small room just off the main office. It had a cot, a small refrigerator, and a shelf full of medical supplies. She wagged a finger sporting a rather long red nail.

"Mr. Bent was very firm when he called down. He wants you thoroughly looked after." She got a few sheets of paper towels and ran them under cold water, and told Kallie to hold it on the burn. "One minute on, one minute off. I'll be back in ten to check on you."

Kallie sat on the edge of the cot. She didn't want to think about how many students had lain there ill. It was probably full of bacteria. She couldn't bear the thought of all the microscopic ecosystems thriving there.

She stood and paced, counting the seconds. One minute on. One minute off. One minute on . . .

"This is all Anna's fault," Kallie muttered between tight teeth. She had put the box completely out of her mind until Anna had brought it back up. And now here it was again, whirling round her head.

The box. The pieces. The Bunsen burner was

definitely a sort of flaming cylinder. Was it yet another coincidence? Kallie's stomach began to churn.

Mrs. Hewlett had left the door to the health room slightly ajar. Kallie could hear her prattling on with her assistant, the short and curly-haired Miss Mallory.

"Such an awful thing," clucked Mrs. Hewlett.

"No surprise, with what's happened, they'd want to give her a fresh start in a new town . . ." said Miss Mallory.

"Good thing no one knows her here. Much easier that way . . ."

Kallie couldn't help but listen. She loathed gossip. But curiosity was an unfortunate side effect of a scientific mind. She wondered whom they were talking about. She'd seen several new faces in some of the younger as well as the older grades.

"But that Winslow woman? I mean, honestly . . ."

Kallie gasped. The Winslow woman? They were talking about Anna. She slunk closer to the door and opened it a smidge farther.

"Such a lovely girl. I'd take her myself if George would let me," said Mrs. Hewlett. "But you know how he is . . ."

Kallie stood, listening wide-eyed to the rest of the conversation. She had forgotten all about the one minute on, one minute off. Her heart began to flutter in her chest, threatening to fly away.

When the topic shifted to Miss Mallory's new puppy, Spartacus, Kallie stepped backward. Her knees wobbled as she sank down onto the cot. The germs no longer seemed important. Neither did her hand. It had begun to throb, but she paid it no mind.

Science class was finished by the time Mrs. Hewlett put a small bandage over Kallie's blister and dismissed her. She made her way to English class, where everyone had begun working on their dioramas.

As soon as she entered the class, several students, including Anna and Pole, stopped what they were doing. They came rushing toward her.

"Are you okay?" asked Queenie.

"I thought for sure you'd gone to the hospital," said Grace.

"I'm fine," said Kallie, awkwardly brushing away the oglers. "Really."

"Back to work," said Ms. Beausoleil. "It's only a

blister. She's not grown a third arm." She winked at Kallie, who was grateful to slip out of the limelight.

Searching the room, Kallie was pleasantly surprised to see the pillows had been stacked in a giant heap in the back corner and round tables had been brought in. It was still a far cry from the neat rows of desks Kallie preferred, but it was a step in the right direction.

Each table was littered with construction paper, glue, boxes, cotton balls, tissue paper, wood chips, and an inordinate amount of glitter. Anna pulled Kallie to a table with all their purchases plus a shabby shoebox, dented on one side. At least she had remembered to bring everything.

"Come on," said Anna. "We need to get going." She was sculpting something out of clay that may or may not have resembled Mr. Tumnus.

Kallie used a sharp pencil to carve triangles from Styrofoam.

"What are you doing?" asked Anna.

"Making stalagmites and stalactites. What does it look like?"

Anna giggled. "There aren't any of those in Mr. Tumnus's cave."

"Says who? And anyway, my cave is going to be realistic—that's the only reason I agreed to it. And real caves have stalagmites and stalactites."

"Okay," sighed Anna, shaking her head. "I'll make the furniture and the décor."

They worked for some time before Anna leaned in and whispered, "So what are you going to do about the bewitched story bones?"

Kallie had been trying to glue jagged Styrofoam triangles to the ceiling of their shoebox, but they kept falling off. She frowned. "There's no such thing."

"But the Bunsen burner," said Anna. "You know—the flaming cylinder . . ."

"It's the power of suggestion. Just like Pole said. If I hadn't put that thought in your head, you'd never have made the connection."

"Maybe," said Anna. "But aren't you even a bit worried?"

"No," snapped Kallie. She was about to say something else, but then she thought about the conversation she'd overheard. She took a deep breath and exhaled slowly. Her voice softened, and she tried to sound cheerful. "Let's just get to work. We have two periods to complete this ridiculous project, and I don't want to have to spend any more time on it than necessary."

Kallie worked diligently until she got all the stalagmites and stalactites to stick to the inside of the box. It didn't look very cavelike being all white. She'd need to paint it. She kicked herself for not having thought to buy paint and a brush when she had been out shopping with Anna.

Anna kept peering up at Kallie and grinning. She had made an acceptable likeness of Mr. Tumnus as well as a lopsided sofa, a lumpy chair, and a crooked lamp. She set the clay aside to dry.

All the while, Kallie thought about what she'd heard in the office. She thought about what the woman in the shop had said about her sweater. And she thought about the box of bones and the next picture—the coffin.

If there was truly power to suggestion, Kallie hadn't stopped it at all. In fact, like a runaway train, it was gaining momentum.

21

THE REVENANT

Kallie stood on the cracked sidewalk outside the Dollar Basket.

She had convinced Grandpa Jess she needed to return to the shop for paint—which was the truth. Of course, he had offered to go with her, but Kallie claimed it would be much faster, not to mention healthier, if she rode her bike. He seemed genuinely excited she was taking more interest in physical activity as of late.

"I won't be long. And I'll come straight home," she'd reassured him. "It won't be dark for a while yet, and I'm ready for more responsibility. Just like Dad said."

Grandpa Jess had reluctantly agreed. He'd even

dug into his pocket and handed her a ten-dollar bill. Kallie had refused at first, but he had insisted.

Kallie paced the sidewalk, staring at the basket of woven dollar signs over the store. She should hurry, but she hesitated. Questions whirled around inside her head. And yet, a part of her wasn't quite sure it wanted the answers.

She opened the door and entered the store. Disappointment mingled with relief when she saw a young woman at the cash register.

"What can I do for you?"

"Paint," muttered Kallie, scanning the space as though she didn't know where to find it.

"Aisle four," said the young clerk.

The woman Kallie had been looking for was nowhere to be seen. She took a deep breath and then headed toward the aisle with the dusty containers. She located a tub of black and a tub of white, plus a small brush. It was all she needed to make her cave look realistic.

"You're in luck," said the young woman as Kallie placed the items on the counter. "Two-for-one sale on paint today."

Kallie forced a smile as she handed the woman the ten-dollar bill. She took her change and her bag and turned to leave.

"I'd hoped you'd return," said a soft voice.

Kallie spun to see the older woman in purple Crocs staring at her.

Part of Kallie wanted to take her paint and leave, but something held her feet steady. There was an awkward moment of silence, and then the woman took a few paces toward her.

"She loved that maroon sweater, you know. The one you wore the other day."

Kallie could feel her hands trembling and her cheeks getting warm. She nearly dropped the bag of paint. The store around her began to swim.

The narrow aisles that were filled with anything and everything you could think of, the dusty shelves, this woman . . . They had known her. They had known her mother and she, her only child, had not.

"How . . ." was the only word Kallie managed. It came out soft and strangled and full of so many conflicting emotions that Kallie wasn't sure the woman would understand. But she did.

"She worked here," said the woman, her eyes crinkling in a sorrowful smile. "Right before . . ."

"She drowned."

The woman bristled at Kallie's abruptness. She stared long and hard, as though she wanted to say something but couldn't quite find the right words.

"She was a good writer," she said finally. "Sometimes, when there were no customers, she'd read things to me."

Anger flared up inside Kallie, though she didn't know exactly why. Was it because this woman—this stranger—knew her mother better than she did? Or was it the writing again—that part of her mother she'd been trained to loathe. "What *things*?"

"Oh. Mostly poems. Some stories. She had a wonderful imagination. And a way with words." She smiled. "I've kept them. I'd be happy to dig them up for you."

Kallie backed away as though the woman were offering her a poisoned apple. There was so much more she wanted to ask. About how her mother had come to work in this shop. About the days leading up to her drowning.

Kallie glanced at her watch. She'd been in the shop longer than she'd promised Grandpa Jess. He would worry.

"I have to go," she said, clutching the plastic bag tightly. She turned to leave but then stopped suddenly and added, "Maybe. If you find them . . ."

The woman smiled and nodded. "I'll have a look."

Kallie found Grandpa Jess in the kitchen making bacon-and-cheddar biscuits for what he called his lazy-day dinner.

"Did you get everything you need?" he asked, slipping the baking sheet into the oven and placing the bowl into the sink. He turned and saw the bag she carried with the Dollar Basket logo and the look in her eyes. He sunk into a seat at the table as though the weight of the world had forced him down.

Needles weren't half as sharp as Kallie's glare. She plunked herself beside him. "Why didn't you tell me?"

Grandpa wrung his hands. Bits of dried dough crusted off. "Tell you what?"

"That she worked at the Dollar Basket."

"Well, what was there to say?"

"I don't know," said Kallie. "But at least I'd know something about her."

"Those weren't good days. Your mother didn't like working there. In fact, she hated it. Your father thought it would be good for her, though. To have some structure to her days. To help out financially."

"He forced her?"

"Forced is such a harsh word, Kallie."

"But she was unhappy."

"It's complicated. Life isn't as neat and tidy as you'd like it to be. It's not black and white. More like shades of gray."

Grandpa Jess stood and went to the sink. He turned on the faucet and began washing his hands. "They were going to see a lawyer. In Plattsburgh."

A lawyer, thought Kallie. It was all he needed to say. It could mean only one thing. Divorce. Her parents were going to divorce. And divorce usually meant a fight—a costly fight over property. Over money. Over children. But then her mother drowned. And a divorce was no longer necessary.

"I smell biscuits," said Victor Jones, stepping into the kitchen. He put his arm around Kallie and gave her a squeeze. "Delicious, but loaded with fat."

"Haven't you heard?" said Kallie. "Fat is now the sixteenth food group."

22

SHADES OF GRAY

The leaves had begun to turn, transforming the mountains from green to gold. In Vermont, the first sign of color change begins mid-September and runs through October, varying by elevation. It progresses from north to south, from higher to lower, until, with three-quarters of the land forest, it is as though the whole state has caught fire, exploding in red, orange, and yellow flames.

Kallie measured one-third cup of white paint and poured it into a plastic cup. She added just the right amount of black—not a drop more, not a drop less—and stirred.

She began painting the Styrofoam stalagmites and stalactites of her cave. With each layer, she added more black to the mixture until the whole interior was undulating shades of gray.

Before Kallie had received the puzzle box, her world had been in perfect order. In perfect balance. Everything had fit neatly into its own special space. Everything had been right or wrong. Black or white.

Kallie stared at the paint already crusting on her paintbrush. Nothing in her perfect world fit into its tidy compartment anymore. Her mother's drowning. Anna. The box. Everything had overflowed and spilled out and mixed sloppily in her mind. Grandpa Jess was right. Kallie's life was now murky shades of gray.

Anna placed Mr. Tumnus and the other objects inside the shoebox and set it proudly on a table at the back of the class. The project was finished.

Much to Kallie's dismay, the other tables had been removed and the pillows had been dispersed about the room once again. Kallie grudgingly sat between Pole and Anna as Ms. Beausoleil picked up a stubby piece of chalk and etched one word on the blackboard.

Hero.

"It's now your turn to write a story," said Ms. Beausoleil. She wore a black lace catsuit under a full-length shawl belted in the center and trimmed in bluish-green peacock feathers. "A hero's journey."

Kallie cringed. "I can't write . . . I'm not a writer." She had meant to say it quietly, to Pole and Anna, but the words had come out a bit too loud.

"Nonsense, Kallie." Ms. Beausoleil pounded her fist on a stack of old leather-bound books piled high on the ground beside her. The goose-fat-colored pages coughed dust with each assault. "Anyone can write, my dear. The trick is to write well."

A feather entered her mouth. She blew it back out and began drawing a diagram on the board. It was a large circle divided into three parts, resembling a mathematical pie graph. It put Kallie slightly at ease.

The teacher labeled the three sections *Act 1, 2,* and *3.* Then she divided each section into three more and gave those titles as well, things like *Call to Action, Mentor, Temptation,* and *Dark Moment.*

Kallie sighed. To her, the words may as well have

been gibberish, but when Ms. Beausoleil began to show how the novel they had just read fit into the formula, she began to understand.

Formula, thought Kallie. Now there was a word she was comfortable with. But a narrative? She'd dodged that bullet over the years, figuring out ways around such assignments. She eyed the teacher, who grinned broadly at the class in her peacock outfit, and something told Kallie the woman would not be as easily dissuaded.

"You must begin with an interesting character," said Ms. Beausoleil, "and you must know their deepest, darkest desires. What does your character want? What do they really desire?"

"To be left alone," muttered Kallie.

"A fine desire. You can work with that," said Ms. Beausoleil. "But you must have a solid plot. One that doesn't meander. Or fizzle. Or crumble like brittle cheese." She scrunched her hands in the air and then dusted them off.

Anna got out a piece of paper and a pen and began jotting down notes.

"You must put your heart into your story—your

blood, sweat, and tears. Every character has bits and pieces of the writer in them to make them flesh and bone so they can walk off the page and live in the minds and hearts of readers."

"Sounds painful," said Pole.

"Oh, it is," said Ms. Beausoleil, nodding fiercely. "Writing is very painful business, indeed. Not for the weak or fainthearted."

"I'm writing about Champ," said Anna proudly. She glanced at Kallie, then at Pole, and smiled.

"Lovely, dear," said the teacher. "There are so many tired old tales. We could use a fresh one."

"Champ is nothing more than a figment of people's imagination," said Kallie.

"He's not," insisted Anna. "He's real."

"He's a tourist trap," argued Kallie. "How could something that large elude capture for so long? Utter nonsense."

"Yes, that's it," said Ms. Beausoleil. "I adore a good debate."

Anna narrowed her eyes, determined. "What about frozen frogs?"

"Frozen frogs?" said Kallie. "What do frozen

frogs have to do with anything?" Anna had a way of twisting a conversation so that the listener had to practically be an acrobat to keep up.

"I have a theory."

"I love theories," said Pole.

The whole class, including Kallie, listened intently as Anna explained.

"If the lake was formed from melting glaciers that carved it out as they moved along this area," said Anna. "Then what if a prehistoric creature that had been frozen during the ice age ended up here—and then like a frozen frog it possessed the ability to rejuvenate itself once the temperature allowed. It thawed and has lived here ever since." She raised her eyebrows and grinned victoriously.

Kallie rolled her eyes.

"A solid hypothesis," said Pole. "Champ does resemble a plesiosaur."

"Well said, Anna. But just be sure your story is thick and juicy," said Ms. Beausoleil, "with plenty of fat for the readers to chew on. A story without meat is nothing but bone."

A spidery shiver crawled up Kallie's spine.

The final bell sounded, ending a most painful day. Kallie gathered her things and stood waiting for Grandpa Jess at their usual spot. Anna and Pole stood at the entrance passing out *Support Periodic Table Day* flyers.

Kallie observed them, checking her watch as each minute passed. She waited and waited, but Grandpa didn't arrive.

23

THE COFFIN

Liah could endure the horror no longer. She sprang from behind the shrubs prepared to fight. She would battle the lot of them—the guards, the drunken guests, the Empress herself—but before she could make a move, she met the bone carver's gaze.

He startled at the sight of her, but his surprise quickly turned to fear. He shook his head, and, as always, Liah understood his gesture. Despite the rage and sorrow filling her insides, she knew then there was nothing she could do to help him. He had chosen his fate, and she could not alter it.

For a long while it seemed there was not enough air in the world to fill her lungs. She stood alone, small and un-noticed, gasping for breath. The sights and sounds and smells seemed to fade, and it was as though she were once again alone in the world.

Memories shifted like shadows in Liah's mind. She had been very young when the bone carver had taken her in. She recalled little of that time. Though, what had never left her were the feelings—feelings of desperation and utter despair as she wandered the countryside, then feelings of safety and security when the bone carver discovered her. He had fed her, had given her shelter, had instructed her in the mystical skill of carving, and now, all she could do was stand idly by and watch him perish.

Suddenly, Liah's eyes fell on the bone carver's sack. She would not abandon that, too. While all attention was on the flaming cylinder, she crept toward it, gathered it up, and slipped back into the shadows. Clutching the cloth tightly to her chest, breathing in its familiar scent, she began to softly weep.

When at last the fire was extinguished, the Empress's voice rang out. "Let the bones cool. Then place them in a box. Hang it for all to see. Their spirits shall know no rest."

The cruel words startled Liah to her senses. She wiped the hot tears from her face as her anguish turned once again to anger. She would avenge her master. She would find a way to win back his bones. Only then could she perform the rituals to release his spirit and give him rest. As Liah waited, she devised a plan.

When a wooden box was placed before the Empress, Liah summoned her courage and stepped out from her hiding place once more. She walked calmly toward the Empress. Bowing low, she opened the sack and offered up the exquisite gifts.

Captivated by the unparalleled beauty of the carvings, the Empress requested a butterfly hairpin be brought to her. She held it gleaming in the waning light of dusk, its gossamer wings so light they might come alive and fly away.

"In exchange for these treasures, I ask only for the bones," she said, pointing to the flaming cylinder.

"And what if I refuse?" said the Empress plainly. "I do not need your permission to keep these treasures. I offer payment out of kindness, not by command."

"You may keep the carvings, it is true," said Liah slyly. "But if you give me what I ask, I shall return with a most precious carving. One worthy of true greatness."

The Empress gazed long and hard into Liah's eyes. Liah thought it might be a pleasing face were it not for the severity in her eyes. Even her hair was pulled tightly off her face, stretching her skin to the limits of elasticity. Then the Empress smiled, but as she did, it was all the more frightening.

"Take the bones, if you so desire."

Liah breathed a sigh of relief, but then the Empress added, "Only, do not disappoint me. If you fail to return, or if your gift is less pleasing than your promise, you and your entire village shall pay for the insult."

Liah thought about all the women and children in her village. She wished them no harm. But she would not let the bone carver's death go unchallenged. She accepted the Empress's terms.

When at last the pyre had cooled, the guards began sifting through the ashes. But after a moment, they drew back, muttering excitedly among themselves. The Empress bade them explain.

"Something strange and unnatural is at work," said one of the guards, "for in this ash is the bones of one man, not two. The other has disappeared."

24

A Mysterious Illness

A chilly gust of wind came out of nowhere, nearly knocking Kallie over. More than fifteen minutes had passed. The after-school crowd had dispersed. Only a few stragglers still milled about, waiting to be picked up.

Pole had left, and Anna waved to Kallie as she slung her backpack over her shoulder, tucked her chin against the wind, and headed up Main toward South Prospect.

Kallie checked her watch again. Seventeen minutes. It wasn't at all like Grandpa to be late. She was growing more impatient and angry by the minute, but when her father's old, reliable gray Malibu pulled up in front of the school, Kallie knew immediately something was wrong. Her father never left work early.

"Quickly," he said, once the car came to a safe stop.

Kallie hopped into the front seat, yanked the door shut, and clicked in her seat belt. "What's wrong? Where's Grandpa Jess?"

Her father talked. She could see his lips moving. She heard the deep, familiar hum of his voice reverberate in her ears. Yet his words seemed to hover like a cloud in the air between them, refusing to sink into her brain. Only one word made its way through the haze.

Hospital.

"Is he . . .? Will he be . . .?" She barely choked out the words before hot tears spilled down her cheeks, dripping onto the satchel she clung to, leaking into the creases and ruts.

"I don't know, honey," said her father gravely. He was calm, but his hands gripped the steering wheel so tight his knuckles turned pearly white. "Mrs. Shepherd saw him lying on the porch steps. She called an ambulance and then phoned me immediately."

The Malibu made it to the hospital in no time at all. It was the first time Kallie had seen her father drive even slightly over the speed limit. That—plus the wind was at their back, giving them an extra nudge. They parked and raced side by side through the emergency doors.

The nurse at the desk gave Kallie's father instructions as to where to locate Grandpa Jess. He turned to Kallie, held her shoulders firmly, and told her she had to stay in the waiting room until he assessed the situation. Kallie's protests went unanswered as her father entered the large doors to the emergency-care unit, leaving her behind.

Minutes passed like hours as Kallie sat rigid in the cold hospital seats, eager for news. When her father finally reemerged from the metal doors, his expression was grave.

"He's in intensive care."

"H-he's going to be all right, isn't he?"

"The doctor isn't sure," said her father. "He's checked him thoroughly but hasn't determined exactly what's wrong. Possibly a heart attack or stroke . . . but the doctor says it's odd, because

Grandpa has tested negative for both and his symptoms don't seem to match any particular illness . . ."

Kallie scanned her memory files for information. A cerebral vascular accident—otherwise known as a stroke—occurred when poor blood flow resulted in the death of important brain cells. A heart attack was a blockage of blood flow to the heart. Both could be fatal.

"Can . . . Can I see him?" She fought back tears.

"The doctor has ordered several more tests to try to get to the bottom of things. When the tests are complete, we can both go in."

"Why can't they figure out what's wrong?" she asked, but the answer was lying deep inside her, waiting for her consciousness to lift it to the surface.

When at last she was allowed in to see him, Kallie found Grandpa Jess lying on a stretcher surrounded by gray curtain walls. He was attached to several monitors that blipped and beeped intermittently. His eyes were closed.

Kallie's tongue felt as heavy as stone when she tried to speak. There was so much she wanted to say. "Oh, Grandpa."

At the sound of her voice, his eyes opened slightly. They were dull. Their usual spark was barely a flicker.

Kallie wanted to throw her arms around his neck and hug him tightly, but she was afraid she'd disturb the various wires and tubes connecting him to the machines. He looked like a tangled puppet. All she could do was slip her hand gently into his and squeeze.

She took a deep breath and frowned. "You were late," she said firmly. Though his eyes closed again, she thought she saw his lips curl into a faint smile.

Kallie and her father stayed at Grandpa Jess's side until the nurse came and told them visiting hours were over long ago. She said there was nothing they could do for Grandpa Jess but let him rest. She reassured them she would take very good care of him.

"Please, Grandpa," Kallie whispered in his ear before she left. "You need to get better. I need those recipes."

Kallie's stomach rumbled loudly in the car as they headed home. She hadn't eaten anything since lunch. Her father offered to stop and pick up a burger—he never bought her fast food—but she declined. No matter what her stomach was saying, she couldn't eat a bite.

It was very late when Kallie got into her pajamas. She was about to turn out the lights when she saw the box sitting on her desk. The waxing crescent moon was on the bottom, and the two stars were on top. It now looked like a sad face.

Kallie trembled as she reached for it. The next piece had been a coffin. "This is all my fault . . ."

"What's all your fault?" her father said, entering the room and startling her. His gaze swung like a metronome between Kallie and the box.

"Grandpa Jess. It's all my fault. You were right. I should never have opened this box."

"I don't see how opening the box has anything to do with Grandpa Jess."

Like a crumbling dam that could no longer hold, Kallie's words rushed out of her in a deluge of battered syllables and raw emotion. Her father's eyes grew tighter and narrower as she spoke.

"Are you quite finished?" he snapped. "Honestly, Kallie. Get a hold of yourself. I've never known you to be so foolish. Grandpa Jess is sick. It has nothing to do with that box."

Kallie swiped at her eyes. "I didn't believe it at first, either . . . but now . . ." If only she had listened to Anna and done something about the box before it had gone this far.

"Nonsense." His voice was growing in strength and velocity. His words crackled like fireworks. "Nothing that has happened has anything to do with that box. All it's done is put irrational ideas into your head."

He wrenched it from her hands, and though she grappled for it, he held it out of reach.

"I'm going to do what I should have done in the first place," he said, his voice flat and cold. "Just as soon as I get a chance, I'm going to pitch this thing into the deepest part of the lake, where it will sink and never be seen again!"

Kallie froze. She stopped reaching. As they stared at each other, her father's expression seemed so hard. Nearly distorted. Kallie had never seen this side of him. He was always calm. Level. In perfect control.

His words seemed to echo inside her. Pitch the

box into the deepest part of the lake . . . Never be seen again . . . Kallie gulped.

He turned to exit the room. "You'll see," he called over his shoulder. "You'll feel much better once this box is out of your life for good."

She could hear his footsteps cross the hall. There was a soft *thunk*, and then she heard his closet door creak shut.

25

ENTANGLED

Kallie spent the next morning at the hospital. Grandpa Jess lay unresponsive in intensive care. The doctor said he had run a battery of tests but could not figure out what was wrong with the man. He looked so pale and emaciated, Kallie thought, as though he were nothing but skin and bone.

The next piece, she thought, panic-stricken, was a skull. She simply had to figure out how to stop whatever was happening. Before it was too late.

She had wanted to spend the entire day by Grandpa Jess's side, but her father insisted there was nothing she could do and she should go to school. She decided he was right—she could not help Grandpa

Jess by sitting there. She had to figure things out, and quickly, and for that she needed help.

As she followed her father out of the emergency area, a nurse stopped her.

"Is your name Kallie?" she said.

Kallie nodded. Her father was focused on the parking payment. He hadn't heard and kept walking.

"I was on duty last night." She smiled warmly. "While I was changing his IV bag, your grandfather regained consciousness for a short time. He kept saying your name over and over. *Kallie. Tell Kallie.* I reassured him I would so he might calm himself."

Kallie swallowed her upset. "What did he want you to tell me?"

The nurse tilted her head. "It didn't make any sense to me, but maybe it does to you. He said, *escape sparky*. Does that mean something?"

Kallie thought about it. "The *Escape* is his boat. I'm not sure what he meant by *sparky*."

The nurse put a hand on her shoulder. "I hope he recovers quickly."

Hopefully, Kallie thought. But all she could

picture was the skull carved into the next piece. A skull. And then a dagger. And then . . . nothing. Her insides quivered with apprehension.

"What did the nurse want?" asked her father as they got into the Malibu.

"She said Grandpa had spoken in the night. He said my name and to tell me: *escape sparky*. Does that mean anything to you?"

Her father frowned and shook his head. "At least he spoke. That has to be a good sign. I'll head back there later and see if the doctor can tell me anything more."

———————— · • · ————————

Kallie arrived at school at lunchtime. She made a bee-line for Pole and Anna.

"I heard," said Pole, putting a hand on her arm. "I'm sorry."

Anna nodded sadly. "Me too. Will he be okay?"

Kallie knew Pole would not like what she was about to say—she may even risk losing him as a friend—but she had to tell them she was now certain it was all somehow connected to the box.

"I told you!" said Anna. "It's those bewitched bones!"

Kallie expected Pole to refute the idea, but instead he shocked her by saying, "I've been giving this careful thought. Ever since you told me about the box and their pieces. There is always a scientific explanation for things. And I think I may have it."

Kallie's eyes widened in anticipation and gratitude, as did Anna's. If Pole could find a logical, scientific explanation for all that had been happening, that meant there would be a logical, scientific way to correct things.

"You've become *entangled*," he said solemnly.

Entangled. Kallie searched her memory. She had read about this phenomenon in the textbook Pole had lent her on quantum physics. "Entanglement? But— that's all just theoretical, isn't it?"

"What's entanglement?" asked Anna. "It sounds awfully painful."

"It's like this," said Pole. "The universe is made of matter. All matter is made of particles."

Anna looked slightly insulted. "I know all about atoms."

"Particles are even smaller than atoms—they're what make up atoms," said Kallie. "Protons, electrons and neutrons . . ."

"*Entanglement*," said Pole, "is a word used to describe how particles of energy and matter can become connected to one another. Even if they are far apart in time as well as space, two particles can interact with each other in a strange and predictable way."

"That's weird," said Anna.

"It's spooky," said Pole.

Anna nodded. "Yeah. Ghostly."

"Not ghostly," corrected Pole. "Spooky. It's actually a scientific term. *Spooky action*."

Kallie's whole body slumped as it all started to make sense. She sighed heavily. "I've become entangled."

"With a story," said Anna excitedly.

"But, how did I get entangled in the first place?"

Pole shook his head. "I don't know. Unfortunately, life is a game of chance, played by quantum physics' rules."

"Okay, then," said Kallie, letting it all sink in, "so how do I get un-entangled?"

"When my hair gets really dirty and it's a knotted mess," said Anna, "I use a detangler. One of those sprays that make the comb glide right through even the toughest knots and undo them."

Kallie and Pole stared blankly at her.

"It's simple, don't you see?" she continued. "What you need is some sort of quantum physics detangler."

26

FLESH AND BONE

Kallie spent all afternoon thinking about what Pole had said and about how she could get herself and Grandpa Jess un-entangled.

"What's all this Tom Brady nonsense?" Ms. Beausoleil stopped Kallie at the end of English class. She held the rough draft of the writing assignment Kallie had turned in. "I had asked you to write a hero's journey."

"I'm not a football fan," said Kallie flatly. "But you have to admit, Tom Brady is pretty much New England's greatest hero since Paul Bunyan."

"Yes, well, unfortunately we are still quarreling with Michigan and Minnesota over the ownership of Mr. Bunyan."

"Not to mention California," said Kallie.

"No, no, no." Ms. Beausoleil waved her neon-blue-polished nails as though swatting invisible flies. "Everyone knows California has no legitimate claim to the lumberjack . . ."

"May I please go now?" said Kallie.

"You may not," said Ms. Beausoleil. She fanned the pages recklessly. "What you have written here is a biography. A list of facts. Not a story. I don't care if Mr. Brady has won a Super Bowl . . ."

"Six."

Ms. Beausoleil stopped. She looked at Kallie vaguely.

"He's won six," said Kallie. "Or is it seven?"

Ms. Beausoleil sighed. "I don't care how many Super Bowls, dishes, forks, or knives Mr. Brady has won, I didn't ask you for a biography. I asked you to write a story. A narrative. A hero's journey. Like *The Odyssey*. Or *The Hobbit*. Or *Beowulf*."

Now it was Kallie's turn to stare blankly.

"Never mind," Ms. Beausoleil said. "We've discussed the structure. I drew a diagram, for heaven's sake."

"But . . . I don't write stories. I told you. I can't. I only write facts," said Kallie coldly. "Stories are lies. I write the truth."

The teacher seemed taken aback. She stopped, and a look of concern creased her brow. Something about her had changed. Her frazzled state seemed to dissolve, and she deflated a bit.

"I see," said the teacher softly. "But I'm afraid you've got something terribly wrong." She placed a gentle hand on Kallie's shoulder and looked her deep in the eye. "Truth doesn't lie nestled snugly within fact. It runs wildly through it, it dances around it, and wriggles in its frayed fringes. Never make the mistake of believing *truth* is synonymous with *fact*, my dear. They are not the same thing."

"But," said Kallie, "a fact is a reality that can't be disputed. Doesn't that make it a truth?"

"No," said Ms. Beausoleil quietly. "A fact is something that simply is. A truth is something that must be discovered. Or created."

"You can't create truth," said Kallie. "That makes it a lie."

The teacher sighed again. She seemed to search the air for a way to explain. "Think of it like this . . . Fact is a series of notes written on a sheet of music. Truth is the melody sung from the heart. Fact is a recipe consisting of ingredients, measurements, and instructions. Truth is the cake that melts in your mouth. Fact is something that happens. Truth is our response to it. Truth tells us who we are. Stories are not lies, Kallie. Stories are the truth in our humanity."

Kallie frowned. She stared hard at the teacher. Ms. Beausoleil seemed suddenly so small. So real.

And then, before she could stop herself, Kallie leaned in and whispered, "What if I do know a story, but I don't know how to end it? Can you help me?"

"That depends." Ms. Beausoleil's eyes glistened with intrigue. "What type of story are we talking about? Is it a comedy? A tragedy? Comedies begin out of order and fall into place. In tragedies, everything slowly falls apart . . ."

"Definitely a tragedy," sighed Kallie.

"Oh," said Ms. Beausoleil gravely. "Well, I hate to tell you, but tragedies usually end in death."

"Death?" gulped Kallie.

"I'm afraid so."

"And that's the only way it can end?"

"There are all sorts of good endings to stories, Kallie. Just remember, a good ending leaves the audience satisfied, with lots to think about. And sometimes, it even comes full circle. It ends right back where it began . . ."

"Back where it began," Kallie echoed. The wheels in her head began to turn. "Thank you," she said genuinely. "Thank you so much. You've been a big help. I'd better go now. I'm late for Mr. Bent's class."

"You? Late for Mr. Bent's class? Now that's a tragedy."

Kallie smiled and was about to leave. But then she stopped and turned back to face the teacher. "You don't happen to have the other books in that series, do you?"

Ms. Beausoleil smiled. "Would you like the first, which is actually the sixth, or the second, which is actually . . ."

"All of them."

Ms. Beausoleil nodded. "I'll dig them up. You'd

best run along now or Mr. Bent will send out a search party."

Kallie grinned. As she dashed from the room, she heard Ms. Beausoleil say, "Remember—a good story never really ends. It lives on inside you forever."

— •●• —

Everyone was already steeped in algebraic equations by the time Kallie entered math class. She tried to join in, but something Ms. Beausoleil had said wormed its way inside her mind. *Sometimes, a story ends right back where it began . . .*

"I need to return the box to the faceless man," she said to Anna and Pole as they gathered their things and walked toward their lockers.

"Of course!" said Anna. "That's it. Return the box to where it came from. That just might do it."

"But where are you going to find him?" asked Pole.

Kallie sighed. "That's the problem. I have no idea."

"I do." Anna grinned. "With a little help from the War of 1812."

"Anna, please," said Kallie. "This is serious."

"I am serious. This weekend is Plattsburgh's commemoration of the War of 1812."

"Hate to tell you this," said Pole, "but that was last weekend."

"No," said Anna. "Labor Day was so early this year and since the actual battle took place on September 11, which is tomorrow, they decided to hold the commemoration this coming weekend. I read about it in the newspaper."

"I know all about the commemoration," said Kallie, waving a dismissive hand. "Grandpa Jess and Grandma Gem used to participate in the reenactment. But what does that have to do with finding the faceless man?"

"Well, on Sunday there's a children's old-time village fair in Trinity Park. You can do all sorts of things, like learn how to make candles, use old tools . . ."

"How is candle making going to help?" asked Pole.

"I was getting to that," said Anna. "There's also going to be a petting zoo and music and all sorts of buskers. The article said a lot of the same performers from the Festival of Fools are going to be there."

"Really?" said Kallie excitedly. "That's great news!"

"I'll go with you," said Anna. "I know my way around these sorts of events. My parents were magicians after all, remember?"

Kallie's eyes met Anna's and held them. "Yes. I remember."

"I can't make it on Sunday," Pole said sadly. "Alejandro is getting an award. We have to drive to New Hampshire for the ceremony."

"We can do it alone," said Anna. "I'll meet you in front of the school bright and early Sunday morning. The children's festival runs from ten until two. We should get there as early as we can."

"Won't Mrs. Winslow mind?" Kallie continued to eye Anna intently.

"Um, no. Of course not," said Anna. "Mrs. Winslow is so busy with all her charitable events and such that she likes it when I have something to occupy my time. She encourages adventure."

"How will you get there?" asked Pole.

"We'll take the island line trail. We'll cross the causeway on the bike path and take the bike ferry to South Hero," said Anna. "From there, we'll take the ferry from Grand Isle to Plattsburgh."

Kallie gulped. The ferry to Plattsburgh. No way. She couldn't. She was about to refuse, but then the image of Grandpa Jess withering away in the hospital bed changed her mind.

"Bright and early," she said to Anna. "And this time, don't be late."

———— •●• ————

Kallie's father picked her up after school and took her to the hospital. Grandpa Jess was still in intensive care. He looked paler and thinner. He was getting worse. Several doctors had examined him, and all remained stumped as to what the mysterious illness could be. They'd ruled out so many things that they were running out of ideas.

Kallie sat all evening with Grandpa Jess. She visited him Thursday and Friday and most of the day Saturday, only stepping out briefly for some fresh air and to run a quick errand. While she held his hand, she told him about school and her biography of Tom Brady, and at one point, she imagined he squeezed her hand. The doctor said it was most likely a reflex. Sunday could not come quick enough.

"I'm going to fix this, Grandpa," she whispered into his ear before she left. "I promise."

It was late Saturday night by the time she and her father got home. The next morning she was to meet Anna at the school, but first she needed to get the box. Her father had placed it in his closet—she hoped with all that was going on, he hadn't had time to get rid of it.

As her father busied himself on his computer, Kallie slipped up the stairs and into his room. Slowly, she creaked open his closet door. Lying on the floor was the box. The full moon and stars were facing her as though with a look of shock and surprise. She scooped it up quickly and held it tightly in her hands. She was about to shut the door when something in the air began to change.

27

THE SKULL

It was late when the Empress gave leave to Liah with the bones of her master and the promise that would seal both their fates.

As she plodded down the mountain, she could not help staring up at the wooden boxes that clung desperately to its side. In them lay all the unfortunates bound to the earth for eternity, never to know rest.

With each step, Liah's resolve and anger grew. First, she would avenge the bone carver's death, and once she had accomplished that, she would return for the others. She would perform the ceremony for each one and send the spirits to eternal peace.

The journey back home seemed longer. The bone

carver had been the only family Liah had known. Now, she had been orphaned once again.

The sky above turned a deep sapphire dotted with starlit spangles. She passed the rocky terrain and the dry fields and arrived at the crossroads. Though she intended to walk the entire way without stopping, she sat at the campsite to rest and to think.

Chewing bitterly on a piece of millet cake, she thought about all that had transpired. Though it had been only the previous night that she had sat with the two men eating meat and listening to the bone flute, it seemed far back in her memory, as though it had happened in another lifetime.

Liah ran her hands along the goatskin shoes, the final gift the bone carver had given her. There would be no rest for her master until the rituals were performed, so she, too, would not rest. Weary, she dragged herself to her feet, and, leaving the clearing, she entered the dark woods.

No starlight penetrated the thick canopy of decaying foliage, so she walked in darkness. The fear swelling in her chest was dulled by the numbness left by her loss. Only when Liah passed the spot where the white beast had leaped at her did she feel a twinge of fear, recalling both it and the shimmering pile of bones.

It was then she suddenly remembered she still carried the skull that she had sworn to return to the forest. She fished it out of her sack and held it up. It caught a sliver of moonlight and glowed an eerie silver. Slowly, Liah left the path in search of the other bones, hoping she would not again lose her way.

As she walked farther and farther into the darkness, she heard a soft sound. She spun round, fully expecting the white beast, only what she saw was far more frightening.

28

In the Closet

The room began to dim, and the air suddenly smacked of moss and decay.

When Kallie looked back at the inside of the closet, something had changed. Beyond the door, where a moment ago all her father's clothes hung in neat and tidy rows, was a darkness that seemed to stretch out infinitely.

I must be dreaming, she thought. Kallie closed her eyes, and gripping the box in one hand, she reached out the other. Surely it would stop once she felt a seersucker sleeve or crisp cotton shirt, but her hand extended farther and farther, meeting nothing. She nearly tipped over, caught her balance, and opened her eyes.

The darkness had enveloped her. Ghostly gray shapes rose up on either side, crooked and looming like tall trees. Before her lay a mass of shimmering white. Her glasses had fogged, but she was still sure of what she saw. A pile of bones.

Kallie took a step backward. She opened her mouth to scream, but before any sound could emerge, a flash of white leaped out, hurdling over her.

It was the white animal Kallie had seen in the middle of the street, what now felt like so very long ago. It came out of nowhere and landed with a *thud* on the hard ground. The beast scrambled to its feet, shook itself, gave her one last look, and then bounded off into the shadows.

Kallie squeezed her eyes tight. She was hallucinating again. She stood frozen for a moment, then mustered all her courage, reached out a trembling hand, and found the hard, flat surface of the closet door. She slammed it shut with a hollow *bang*.

"What's going on up there?" said her father.

"N-nothing," said Kallie, the blood beating in her ears. She opened her eyes. She was in her father's room. All was still and quiet. It no longer smelled of rot and decay, but faintly of his aftershave.

It's that Narnia book, Kallie thought, scowling. And the box. They had infected her brain like a disease. She must have imagined it all—the white beast, the pile of bones, the shadowy world beyond the closet door. Nonsense. Folly.

She took a deep breath, gripped the doorknob firmly, and opened it again. All her father's clean suits and crisply ironed shirts hung neatly in their place. Nothing was out of place. She exhaled.

Footsteps creaked across the downstairs hall.

Kallie startled. She had to get out of the room quickly. Her father would be up any moment. If he caught her with the box, she didn't know what he might do. She gripped the door handle firmly, but before she swung it closed again, she caught sight of something. Another box. Only this one was large, made of cardboard, and filled with paper and a large manila envelope with something scrawled on the front.

Kallie scrambled back into her room, hiding the

box in her satchel as her father climbed the steps. She got changed and climbed into bed.

"Were you happy?" she asked when her father came in to check on her. "You and Mom?"

"What?" he said, looking upset and bewildered. "What makes you ask that?"

"I don't know," said Kallie, fumbling with her covers. "I've just been wondering."

He sighed. "That was a long time ago, Kallie. It doesn't matter anymore."

The look on his face gave her the answer his words would not.

Kallie lay in bed, but sleep would not come. All she could think about was the white beast, the shimmering pile of bones, and Grandpa Jess lying in the hospital bed wasting away.

And about the two words on the envelope in the box in her father's closet:

Insurance policy.

29

BENEATH THE SURFACE

The house was silent and still. Victor Jones was long gone. He had told Kallie the night before he needed to set out early for the office to sort out a few things. He promised he would return for her in the late afternoon so they might go to the hospital together.

Kallie sprang out of bed at the sound of her alarm. She'd set it a whole hour and a half early. With no time to waste, she prepared herself quickly, forgoing all her usual routines. And the strange thing was, she didn't seem to miss any.

Getting to Plattsburgh and back by the afternoon was her only focus. It would be difficult at best, if not impossible. She couldn't squander a moment.

Wrapping herself in her mother's maroon sweater,

she slung her leather satchel over her shoulder. In it, she tucked the box. The bones rattled and clattered violently as she fled down the porch steps, as though fighting to get loose.

It was one of those September mornings that reached for autumn with icy fingertips. The cool air quarreling with the still-tepid waters of the lake conjured up a thick, shapeless fog. It rolled off the surface and into town, consuming everything in its path.

Kallie could barely see three feet in front of her as she picked a path around the side of the house toward the garage and got out her bike. Fog pressed in on her from all sides as she made her way toward the school. Though she felt solid and sure on her bike now, she rode extracautiously, stopping at each intersection to make certain it was safe to cross.

Anna was waiting in front of the old building. She greeted Kallie with a cheerful wave. Together they rolled down Main Street toward the lake and the Burlington Bike Path.

The path followed the old Rutland Railroad route. In 1901, the trains trundled passengers and freight from Vermont to western New York and on into Quebec. It was never a solid financial operation, and the company declined steadily until it was abandoned altogether. Eventually a recreational trail was created over the old trestles. The path wound through Burlington, Colchester, and then over a marble causeway toward South Hero.

Kallie had traveled only short distances on the path. She had never ridden all the way along the fourteen-mile trail. After the first few miles, she began to huff and puff, but she pressed herself to continue at top speed because there was little time to spare. Anna rode out ahead, swallowed up entirely by fog. Luckily, her incessant chatter was like a beacon of sound for Kallie to follow.

The path took a sharp turn and left the mainland, continuing out on the narrow causeway over the foggy lake. Kallie paused a moment before venturing onto the single-lane path that disappeared into the fog. She could hear Anna's disembodied voice calling to her but she could no longer see her. She put a shaky foot back on the pedals and began moving onto the path. Glancing over her shoulder, she could no longer see solid land. It was as though she were gliding out of reality and into a dream.

"Slow down," she called to Anna.

"It's like flying over the water!"

"If you're not careful," said Kallie, "you're going to fly *into* the water!" The only response was a soft giggle.

As they continued toward the center of the lake, the fog began to change. It lifted off the surface like a layer of sunburned skin. Then the wind teased it, pulling wisps upward like ribbons of cotton candy, stretching them long and lean, twirling them toward the sky like wispy vines.

"The dance of the steam devils," whispered Kallie.

She had watched this phenomenon many times with Grandpa Jess from the safety of the swinging benches. But out here, on the lake itself, it was as though she had become part of the dance.

Suddenly, she heard Anna screech to a halt. Kallie snapped from her trance and hit her brakes. The path ended abruptly at a little white shelter with a bright-blue sign announcing: WELCOME TO THE

LOCAL MOTION ISLAND LINE BIKE FERRY. They had halted just in time. Another few feet and they might have broken through the barrier and gone into the lake.

The two girls dismounted and headed down the ramp. The ferry arrived in no time. It was a small vessel. They paid their fare, anchored their bikes, and sat opposite each other on white wooden benches. A heavy silence filled the space between them as the ferry dipped and swayed, shuttling them quickly across the two-hundred-foot gap between causeways known as the Cut.

It took only a few minutes. Before she knew it, Kallie had left the ferry and was pedaling on toward Grand Isle and the second ferry—the one that would take them to Plattsburgh. She and Anna purchased their tickets at a small wooden hut, boarded the large ferry along with several cars, and waited for it to leave the dock.

Kallie hadn't been worried on the bike ferry—that was like being out on the *Escape*. But taking this particular vessel was different. A lump began to form in Kallie's stomach as she stared out at the choppy water, thinking. Wondering.

The captain blew the whistle, and the ferry began to drift. Once out on the open water, the boat rocked and swayed. Kallie kept far from the railing, while Anna insisted on hanging over it and looking out. The last vestiges of fog rose from the surface, reaching up with misty tendrils before dissolving into nothing.

"Get away from the edge," warned Kallie, but Anna wasn't paying attention. She had dropped her big backpack onto the deck and was leaning farther over the railing. "Be careful, Anna," Kallie tried again, but the girl paid her no mind, practically dangling over the side.

"Look!" shouted Anna suddenly, pointing and stretching her arms as if to touch something elusive. "It's Champ!"

In one slow, spiraling moment, Kallie watched, paralyzed, as the ferry hit a rogue wave and dipped downward so sharply that Anna lost her balance. She flapped like a sheet in the wind and then flew over the railing and into the dark water, disappearing under the waves.

Was this how it had happened all those years ago?

Had Kallie's mother simply lost her footing? Drowning wasn't the loud, splashy panic people imagine it to be. Kallie had researched it extensively. Drowning was quick and quiet. People just slipped beneath the water and were gone.

Searing and strangled thoughts snapped Kallie back to the moment and spurred her into action. She wasn't going to let Anna slip away from her, too. She let out a guttural cry for help and then jumped into the lake, clothes, satchel, and all.

The air left her lungs as her body smacked the cold water. The lake sucked her downward, but she battled hard, kicking wildly, reversing direction, and losing her shoes in the process. She breached the surface, gasping for air, swallowing greedily.

Her glasses were in place, but it was like trying to see through a rain-soaked windshield. She searched frantically for Anna. In the distance, she glimpsed a head bobbing in the waves. It came up briefly, hands clambering as if to climb an invisible ladder, and then she was gone again.

"Anna!" Kallie screamed, taking in a mouthful

of musky water and gurgling it back out. "Hold on, Anna! I'm coming!"

The leather satchel and wool sweater, saturated and heavy, threatened to drag Kallie back beneath the waves. She disentangled herself from both and began swimming as hard as she could toward the spot she had last seen Anna. Straining every muscle, she struggled against the current. In the distance, she could hear a cacophony of voices coming from the ferry. They had heard her call. That was good.

Kallie's arms and legs ached, but she pressed onward. The head came up once more and then was gone again. But Kallie was close—only about twenty feet away. She swam harder, her muscles burning, until she reached Anna, who was now facedown in the water. This was a good thing, because a panicked victim could turn the would-be rescuer into a second victim.

Kallie thrust her arms under Anna's. She lay back, bringing Anna's head above the water. She began to whip-kick toward the ferry, which had stopped. Two men had jumped into the lake as well and were heading toward them with a flotation device. Kallie was quickly running out of steam. The two men reached her just as Kallie felt herself sinking.

Anna coughed and sputtered water as they were pulled back onto deck. Someone threw a scratchy gray blanket around Kallie's shivering shoulders as she hovered over Anna, watching one of the men check her ABCs—airways, breathing, and circulation.

"I'm fine," Anna insisted. She sat up, grinning. "Really. Just a little wet, but no worse for wear."

The other man handed Kallie her sopping leather satchel. He had fished it out of the water along with her sweater. She had forgotten all about the satchel. And the box.

Kallie opened the satchel and shook it frantically, but it was empty. She cast it aside, despondent.

"I-I'm sorry," said Anna, reaching for her arm.

But it was too late. The box was gone and along with it all hope Kallie might return it to the faceless man.

"Grandpa," she whispered softly.

30

A LIGHT EXTINGUISHED

Despair sunk like a concrete block in Kallie's stomach. Without the box, how would she un-entangle herself?

The Plattsburgh paramedics were waiting on the other side. They checked out Anna and Kallie thoroughly, and even when it was certain both were in excellent health, they insisted parents must be notified.

"No!" shouted Anna and Kallie at once.

"We're fine," said Kallie.

"I swim all the time in the lake," said Anna.

"My father is extremely busy with work. And my grandfather is in the hospital. And we have a very important meeting we are late for . . ."

"So, if you'll be so kind as to shut the doors of the

ambulance and allow us to change into some dry clothes, we'll be on our way . . ."

"Dry clothes?" said Kallie.

"Yes," said Anna. "I always keep extra clothing in my backpack for just such an occasion."

Anna handed Kallie a pair of ruby-red sweat-pants, her yellow T-shirt, and a worn pair of flip-flops. Kallie felt odd—as though she were not just slipping into Anna's clothes, but somehow into Anna. Every-thing was a tad too small and far more color than Kallie was used to. When she was ready, she packed the wet clothing into her now-empty satchel. She took a deep breath and sighed. Returning the box to the faceless man was her only hope of ending her connec-tion to the bones and saving Grandpa Jess.

"Don't worry," said Anna softly, stroking Kallie's arm. "We'll find the faceless man. You can talk to him. He can tell you what to do."

Kallie didn't have the energy to argue. There were only two more pieces. A dagger. And then nothing.

Nothing. As though everything Kallie knew and loved would be gone. As though her life as she knew it would be over. And possibly Grandpa's along with it.

She couldn't waste more time scolding Anna. They were late—soon the children's festival would be over. They had to move quickly.

They thanked everyone again, got on their bikes, and sped off along Margaret Street toward Cumberland. Kallie found it difficult to pedal in the flip-flops, but they had lost valuable time; they couldn't lose any more.

In front of an old, picket-fenced house with a sign that read KENT-DELORD HOUSE MUSEUM, there was a huge commotion. Throngs of people dressed in period costumes and carrying wooden muskets milled about. Kallie overheard someone say they were preparing for a battle reenactment. The crowd was so thick Kallie and Anna were forced off their bikes and had to walk. They stopped only briefly to ask for directions.

They reached Trinity Park with little time to spare. The festivities appeared to be wrapping up. There was a clown making balloon animals, a juggler, a petting zoo with goats and a donkey, and a man walking on stilts. There was a tent set up, and it appeared kids were dipping wax to make candles. There was also a puppet theater with dancing marionettes. Kallie was worried. She didn't recall seeing these performers at the Festival of Fools. They wandered around the park, but there was no sign of the faceless man. If he had been there, perhaps they'd missed him.

"You know," said Anna. "One time, my mother and father were performing at a festival just like this . . . and then someone began . . ."

Frustration welled inside Kallie. "Stop it!" she said sharply. She turned toward Anna, her face contorted with a corrosive anger. "Just stop it!"

Anna flinched, her expression crestfallen.

Kallie continued to glare with withering scorn. She had had enough of Anna and her tall tales. How dare Anna remain impervious to the harshness of reality while Kallie had to face it—every last painful bit?

"I should never have trusted you! You're a liar! None of what you say is true . . ." Her words flew at Anna like angry hornets.

Anna seemed to struggle with what Kallie was saying, with the shape and texture of the words, as though trying to form something solid out of a limp lump of dough.

"You aren't the relative of the long-lost Russian princess. Mrs. Winslow isn't rich. You don't live in a mansion on Prospect. You live in a tiny apartment in the Old North End. You don't have any nice clothes, and you barely get anything to eat."

Tears welled in Anna's eyes. She shook her head slowly. "You don't know what you're saying."

"Yes," said Kallie. "I do. I know exactly what I'm saying. You keep telling everyone your parents are coming home. But they're never coming home. I know it. And you know it. And it's time you face the truth."

Like a marionette with its strings cut, Anna crumpled. She looked at Kallie with a hurt so raw it blistered.

Regret tugged at Kallie, trying to drag her back, but like a runaway train, her mouth kept moving and words kept flying out.

"I heard the secretaries at school talking. I know the truth. I know what really happened. You say your father put your mother in a wooden box—a magical box. Well, he put her in a wooden box and he went in after her all right, only it wasn't a magical box at all!"

Tears streamed down Anna's face. Her expression implored, *Why did you have to say that?* "M-my mother is in a box," she said. "A wonderfully fancy wooden box. You have your truth. I have mine. What makes yours more valid?"

"Your parents are gone," said Kallie. "Just like my mother. I've had to accept it. And so do you. They're gone and they're never coming back. That box you keep talking about—that fancy wooden *magic* box—it's nothing but a plain old coffin."

As Kallie stood there, triumphant in her truth, she saw the bright light that had always shone in Anna's eyes flicker and go dim. Anna didn't react. She didn't respond. She stood staring at Kallie as if the world around her had gone dark.

Kallie remembered the girl she had seen smiling and dancing in the rain. That girl was gone. The girl before her was smaller. Frailer.

The locked box inside Kallie's mind clicked open, and before she could stop it, a memory slipped out. It was of another time and another place. Of another girl dancing in the rain, laughing and stomping through puddles, getting wet and dirty. That girl had been holding her mother's hand. It was all so long ago Kallie had forgotten what it had felt like.

Guilt thumped in Kallie's chest. She had been so large and looming a moment ago, but now she popped like a soap bubble. "Anna, I . . ."

Anna stood. She did an about-face and ran into the crowd.

Kallie was about to go after her when she heard a familiar sound. It was a violin, playing a hauntingly familiar tune. A man on a zigzag unicycle rolled passed her.

31

THE DAGGER

A familiar laughter sprung from the shadows, sharp and clear.

Unable to take in what she was seeing, Liah looked down at the skull in her hands. This was no trick. She had disobeyed the bone carver when she took the piece from the forest. She had disturbed its spirit, and by doing so had brought it along on her journey. And as a consequence of her actions, the bone carver had died. It had been her fault.

As the knowledge sunk in, the laughter around her died and the shimmering figure vanished—swallowed back into the magical shadows that had spat it out.

Liah gazed for a long time at the skull in her hand. She might return it to the forest. She might take it with her and perform the rituals, releasing its spirit. Then she heard the Lie-peddler's own words return to her in haunting clarity.

If my spirit were to be set free, my journey would end. And I have much more to accomplish in this world.

With much more care than the first time, Liah wrapped the skull in silk and placed it in her satchel. She knew now exactly what must be done.

Liah returned home to the village. There was a great cry of sorrow at the news of the bone carver's death and a greater cry of anger at the cruelty and malice of the Empress.

Liah prepared to give the bone carver a proper burial. She began by cleaning and polishing the bones. She arranged them on a bed and repeated the chants she had learned from him. For forty-nine days she made sacrifices to his ancestors, calling on them to come and take his spirit to its eternal resting place.

On the last day, she found a spot in the ground beside his forefathers, buried his bones deep so that no animal might find them, and planted a shrub to grow and flourish above him. Though she and the bone carver shared no blood, Liah now felt she had an ancestor whose grave she might tend and whose spirit might watch over her.

All the while, Liah had also been preparing her revenge. She spent many hours carving something truly special, truly unique. Something that would not only gain the admiration of the Empress but would also bring about her end. When at last all was ready, Liah prepared for her journey back to the palace.

The villagers begged her not to go, for opposing forces had mustered their armies and were sweeping the lands, destroying all those loyal to the Empress.

"I must go," she said to them. "I have promises to keep." And with that, she set out once again for the palace.

Without stopping once, Liah reached the mountains by nightfall. She had plenty of work to do. She set about her business.

By the time Liah entered the palace, it was empty and abandoned. She strode past the thick walls and around to the terrace, where she found the Empress sitting alone. No longer filled with the sound of drunken laughter, it seemed all the more cold. The only light came from the coals beneath the bronze cylinder. The Empress sat mesmerized by the flames, their reflection turning her black pupils red.

Liah stepped forth from the shadows, and the Empress cast her an uninterested glance. "Have you come to fulfill your promise?" she said wryly. "Have you brought me a beautiful carving?"

From her sack, Liah withdrew the box she had taken much time to prepare. She held it toward the Empress. "I have."

A flash of cruelty lit her eyes as she reached for it.

"I know how you enjoy your boxes filled with bones," said Liah. "So I have brought you such a box."

In the distance, Liah heard the thunder of hooves. The opposing army was approaching. Soon they would lay siege.

She watched as the Empress turned the box over. The bones spilled out of the open circle across the stone floor. She placed them in a straight line:

A faceless figure

A large sun

A three-sided shape

A boat

A tunic

A cavern

A serpent

A thin instrument

The Empress picked up the final bone and held it up for Liah to see. It had nothing on it. "Ah, but you made an error. This one has no image."

Liah took a dagger from her sack and set it down at arm's length between them. It was smooth and lean and razor sharp.

The Empress looked at Liah with hooded eyes. A tiny grin snaked across her lips as she understood. "Ah. I see. One of us shall die," she said in a voice as dull and insipid as rain.

Liah nodded. "Yes. One of us."

The Empress glared at the dagger, then at the final piece of empty bone. "The question, then, is: Which of us shall perish and which shall survive?"

Liah picked up all nine bones. She placed them inside the box. The circles spun backward, playing a sweet melody as it sealed tight.

"That decision is not in my hands," said Liah. "Nor in yours. It is beyond both of us now. It lies in the hands of the storyteller."

32

UNMASKED

Kallie saw the belly dancer first. Her thick, embroidered belt jingled and jangled as she rocked and swayed. A little farther along, the fire juggler tossed his flaming sticks high into the air, and next to him the lady in the shimmering blue leotard stood on her hands, shooting arrows with her toes. It took Kallie by surprise, because she hadn't noticed them there a moment before.

These were the same performers she had seen at the Church Street Marketplace. She searched for Anna to tell her the good news when, out of the corner of her eye, she caught sight of a lean figure standing in the shadows in an alley between two buildings. She recognized him immediately.

It was the faceless man.

Slowly, Kallie moved toward him as though he were reeling her in with an invisible line. When she was only a few feet away, he touched the tip of his pink fedora and bowed his head slightly. Despite his lack of features, she was sure he was smiling.

"I've come to return the box . . ." she said, her voice barely a whisper.

The figure stood perfectly still, his featureless face assessing her. Her courage leaked out like water through tissue paper. She gathered what was left of it and continued. "But, I've lost it, you see, and . . ."

He didn't move a muscle. Now more than ever, he reminded Kallie of a mannequin standing motionless in a shop's window display.

She was about to explain further when he shifted. He'd been so perfectly immobile, and the movement so sudden, it startled Kallie. He reached for his fedora, held the hat in one hand, and tapped it lightly with the other.

Out tumbled the box.

He held it in the palm of his hand, his arm outstretched just as he had done the first time.

"But . . ." she whispered. "I saw it sink . . ."

He turned the box over until the blank side faced her—the one with no moon and no stars. What Kallie had thought to be the new moon.

The blank face on the box reminded Kallie of the final piece—the one with all blank faces. She had thought it had meant nothing. Emptiness. The end. She had been wrong.

"It's my story," she said, realizing for the first time the power and potential in those words. "And I must end it."

He tapped his hat again, and something else came out. It was long and lean and pointed on one end. It resembled the second-to-last picture—the one she had decided was a dagger. She had been wrong about that as well.

He held the item toward her. She took it in her trembling hands. She could hear Ms. Beausoleil's words echo in her mind. *A tragedy ends in death . . .*

The man dropped the box inside his fedora and placed it back on his head. Then he turned to leave, but Kallie, gripped with curiosity, cried out, "Wait!"

The man stopped.

"Who are you?" she asked.

All sounds around Kallie ceased. The people at the festival seemed to fade into the background. Nothing existed but Kallie and the man as he slowly turned to face her. And like the slick black skin of a rotting banana, he peeled the flesh-colored material from his face and she saw clearly the ghastly sight that lay beneath.

The face had no flesh. No eyes. Nothing but bone. The skull was covered in carved circles, which turned and spun like clockwork.

Kallie gasped in horror. She glanced around to see if anyone else was witnessing what she was, but when she looked back toward the ghoulish face, the man was gone.

Kallie found Anna sitting on a curb beside the sad-faced clown. She had brought along her ocarina and had joined in his performance. When she saw Kallie, she stopped playing.

Despite the surrounding sounds, a heavy silence seemed to stretch out like a chasm between them.

"Did you find him?" Anna asked at last.

Kallie nodded.

"Is it over?"

Kallie clutched the leather satchel close to her chest. In it was the final item the man had given her. "Almost."

33

Truth and Lies

Kallie's father stood on the porch, his arms folded, his black Oxford shoe tapping a nervous rhythm. A crease deeper than the Grand Canyon divided his forehead.

"Where have you been? I've been sick with worry. And what are you wearing?"

Kallie's heart squeezed up and, for a moment, she could neither move nor stand still. Her head swam with all the things she wanted to say.

"There was something I needed to do . . ." she began, but he cut her off.

"I see. Well, I can't believe you'd be so irresponsible. So unpredictable. So . . ."

"I know the truth," she said suddenly, her voice

so tight the words nearly strangled her. In the distance, she heard a low rumble. Above, the raven-feather clouds were gathering again.

Her father bristled. His eyes narrowed to slits. "What *truth*?"

She trembled with anger and fear, but she held her ground. "The truth about what happened to my mother."

No sooner had the words escaped her lips, than her father turned a ghostly shade of pale. He wobbled slightly and then steadied himself against the doorframe. He looked as though he might be ill.

"Who told you?" His voice was flat, emotionless.

Her father had always been strong and sturdy, as unmovable and unbendable as an old oak tree. His sudden weakness was a shock, but Kallie continued. She raised her chin, firing words at him like pointy darts.

"I heard you talking with Grandpa Jess. You said you did it for my sake. You said Grandpa should let sunken truths stay sunk. I met the woman at the Dollar Basket. I saw the insurance policy."

Her father closed his eyes and took a deep breath. When he opened them, they were dull. Resigned. As though something had drained from them.

"I knew this day might come," he said. "But I'd hoped it wouldn't."

Kallie felt a fury violent and powerful zip through her body. "You *killed her*! You pushed my mother into the lake and she drowned! You got rid of her and just hoped I would never find out?"

Her father startled. His jaw slackened, and his eyes grew as wide as saucers. He looked at Kallie as though she were something grotesque and alien, as though she had just sprouted another head.

The color flooded back into his cheeks, turning them a deep scarlet. He ran his hands through his perfectly combed hair, mussing it. A half smile tugged at the corner of his mouth. "Is *that* what you think?"

"I put all the facts together," said Kallie, her words now like nails meant to catch him and hold him in place. "Everything I heard you and Grandpa Jess talking about. You did it for my sake. You killed her for my sake."

"Come on in," he said softly, holding the door open. "It's time I tell you the truth. The real truth."

Kallie eyed him suspiciously. What sort of trick was this? She'd finally said out loud what she had been thinking for some time, and yet now that the truth was out, it was hard to reconcile the image of her father—the man who had always been there for her, the man who, despite his rigidness, had never so much as hurt a fly—and that of a coldhearted killer.

She clutched the leather satchel close to her chest and followed him inside.

"Sit down," he said, pulling out one of the kitchen chairs and seating himself in another. Tentatively, she slipped into the seat.

"So," he began, looking her straight in the eye. "You believe I killed your mother?"

"Yes," she said firmly. "You had an insurance policy. When I went into your closet to look for the box, I saw it. You were going to divorce, but instead of paying for it, you got rid of her and then got the insurance money."

"That box." He sighed and shook his head. "I

knew it was trouble the first time I saw it. I just knew it would fuel your imagination."

"It's not my imagination. And my mother's drowning has nothing to do with the box."

He tried to reach for her. She leaned away.

"Grandpa Jess warned me, but I didn't listen. He said I would pay for what I'd done. Well, now I suppose that time has finally come. Only it's not what you think."

Kallie wore the damp satchel like a bulletproof vest protecting her from what she was about to hear. Though she had expected his confession to hurt, she was not prepared for what was to come.

"I didn't kill your mother," he said softly. Kallie began to protest, but before she could say a word, he added, "Your mother's not dead."

For one bewildering moment, Kallie struggled to make sense of what her father had said. His words were so calm, so gentle, and yet they were like a punch to her stomach. Kallie felt the wind knocked out of her. Her arms fell limp, and the satchel made a *thud* on the floor. She could barely breathe, let alone manage to get words out.

"No." She shook her head. "You're lying . . . She can't be . . . She's dead . . ."

"She's not," her father repeated. "She's very much alive and living in Montreal."

"No," said Kallie again, grappling to understand his words, but it was like trying to recall a faint melody heard only once. "She can't be . . . She's not . . . She's alive?"

Outside, there was another rumble, and rain came down so hard and so suddenly, it was as if the sky had broken open.

Kallie's father reached for her arm, but she yanked it away. Her thoughts spun like the needle of a compass pointing in one direction. No body had ever been found. Could it possibly be? All these years, had her mother been alive? Kallie looked at her father, and it all suddenly made sense, and it was her turn to feel sick.

She sprang to her feet and raced for the door, bolting out into the pouring rain. She wanted to run. Run and run and never stop.

Her father came after her. He grabbed hold of her arm, pulled her toward him, and held tight. She thrashed and struggled to free herself from his embrace, and when she had not an ounce of energy left to fight, she gave up, exhausted, and he let her go. They stood staring at each other.

"You lied to me," she gasped. "All this time, you've been lying to me." The pouring rain did nothing to quell the fire raging within her.

"No," he said, shaking his head. "Not at first."

He took a step toward her, but she backed away.

"At first," he said, "I believed what she had wanted me to believe—that she had drowned. It was the worst day of my life, Kallie. And it didn't end—it went on and on as they searched for her body and never found her. I thought she was gone forever. I really truly believed it when I told you."

The rain soaked through his suit. His hair flopped down in his face. For the first time, he didn't look perfect. Or in control.

"Maybe it would have been best if it just stayed that way, but it was that insurance policy. They rarely pay out if there is no firm evidence a person is, in fact, gone. They sent investigators, and after a year of searching, they found her. Living in Montreal. With a musician named Claude."

"But . . . how?"

"She must have planned it," he said. "I don't know. One moment she was on the ferry. The next, she was gone . . ."

Kallie couldn't move as the new truth soaked into her bones along with the rain. She couldn't decide what was worse. Her mother dead. Her father a killer. Or that she had been abandoned. Unloved.

Her father reached for her and pulled her toward him. He held her in such a tight embrace she thought he'd squeeze the life out of her.

"She left us, Kallie. Just like that. And you had already done so much grieving. You were so little and so resilient, and you had found a way to live and move on. I couldn't hurt you all over again. I decided to just let you believe she was dead."

"But it's your fault. You made her work at that store. You made her unhappy when all she wanted to do was write."

"Yes. She was unhappy working at the store. And yes, I asked her to do it. But you don't know why."

She looked at him. His eyes filled with a sorrow so deep it seemed bottomless.

"Your mother was different. I loved her with all my heart, but it was like trying to love the sunshine or the wind or the steam devils that dance on the lake. She was never all here. Never all present. Her mind was always somewhere far, far away. One day, I came home from work and found you staggering at the top of the steps in a diaper that hadn't been changed all day. She said she'd simply lost track of time. And it wasn't just once. She did that a lot. Yes, I wanted her to get that job, but so that Grandpa could take care of you . . . so you could be safe and well-cared-for and . . ."

"All my life," said Kallie, blood beating in her ears, "you told me not to believe stories. You told me stories were terrible things. They were lies. And yet you told me the biggest lie of all."

He hung his head, and then she realized it wasn't the rain. For the first time in her life, her father was crying.

Nothing Kallie knew or believed was right anymore. All her memories clattered in her mind, knocking against one another. How could she have believed her father was a killer? How could he have lied to her all these years? Nothing made sense. It was as if her whole world had been made of glass and someone had thrown a giant rock, shattering it.

She had to leave. Had to get away. She turned and prepared to run, but before she could take a step, her father's cell phone rang.

"It's the hospital," he said.

34

A Sort of Ending

September was more than halfway over. The days were quickly evaporating, like steam devils after their last dance across the lake. October would have an entirely different feel to it, thought Kallie as she sat on the swinging bench staring out at the water. Her hair fell loosely at her shoulders. It made her features seem softer.

The surface of the water was calm today. Not even a ripple. It was funny how the lake's mood could change so quickly. Light came and went, swells rose and fell, wind moved in and out. One minute it was calm, the next blustery. And of course the mountains would cast their shadows like nets, trapping boats and islands and possibly other, more ancient things in their snare.

Kallie found herself thinking about the lake. Its history. Its formation. It was home to the oldest fossil coral reef in the world. It was the excavation site of a ten-thousand-year-old beluga whale. Even the youngest mountains flanking its banks were made of rock that had formed over one billion years ago.

Twelve thousand years ago, when the glaciers that had blanketed the area in a mile-thick sheet of ice began to melt, water pooled in the area. The monstrous mountains of ice had been so heavy, they had forced the land below sea level, carving out the lake. Then, as the glaciers receded north, ocean water flowed into the area, which would eventually be replaced by freshwater.

Perhaps, thought Kallie, *Anna is right*. Perhaps like frozen frogs that thawed in spring, something else had come alive when the enormous glaciers had melted. Perhaps there really was a Champ. And perhaps Kallie would see the monster one day.

"You knew," said Kallie. She reached over and

took the hand of the familiar figure sitting beside her. "You knew even before Dad did."

Grandpa Jess wrapped his leathery fingers around her small hand and squeezed. He nodded.

Everyone—especially the doctors—was left in shock. Grandpa had taken ill so suddenly and so violently. And then, as though someone had thrown a switch, he was fit as a fiddle once again.

"That's what you were trying to tell me that day at the hospital," she said. "The *Escape* . . . not *sparky*, but *spare key*. My mother took the spare key, didn't she? Someone was in the boat, waiting to take her to the other side. You figured it out."

A watery skin was formed over Grandpa's eyes. Again, he nodded.

"But . . . why didn't you tell me? I could have handled it."

A tear trickled down his cheek, and Kallie reached over and wiped it. "Because it wasn't my truth to tell."

"You were wrong not to tell me. But it's okay. I understand why you didn't."

He squeezed her hand again, and this time he smiled. "There's such a thing as too much truth."

Kallie thought about Anna. The cruel truth she'd forced her to face. Perhaps Grandpa was right. Perhaps some truths were not universally owned. They were not everyone's to tell.

"I think I understand something else now," she told Grandpa Jess. "Sometimes people need lies. Little lies to help them deal with truths that are too huge and too difficult to face."

"We can't steal those life-lies, Kallie," he said. "Sometimes, like hopes and dreams, they're all some people have."

Kallie paused a moment to think about what Grandpa had said. Truth. Lies. Hopes. Dreams. She reached into her leather satchel she'd brought with her. She took out the old papers filled with scribbled writing. She held them toward Grandpa.

"Her stories," she said. "I got them from the lady at the Dollar Basket on Saturday, while you were still in the . . ." Her voice choked a little on the word *hospital*. "I'm going to read them."

Just then a figure approached. He stood for a moment and then settled down on the swinging bench right between Kallie and Grandpa Jess. He must have left the office early. They stared at one another for a long moment, and then her father spoke.

"How about we read them together?" he said, putting his arm around Kallie and holding her in a firm grip. He smiled, and it was awkward, as though his face muscles were rusty.

A cool breeze blew, lifting her loose hair, dancing it around her face. She smiled back and nodded, and then hugged him, squeezing as many unsaid things into the embrace as she could possibly fit. When she finally let go, they sat together, staring at the lake, talking and laughing.

"I almost forgot," she said as they stood to leave. "I'm staying late after school tomorrow."

Grandpa Jess and Victor Jones each raised a curious eyebrow.

"Mr. Washington asked me to join his elite art class." She looked a bit pleased, a bit perplexed. "He said I've shown some real talent."

———— ·•· ————

Earlier that day, Pole had met Kallie at the front of the school. "How's your grandfather?" he had asked.

"Miraculously better," said Kallie, grinning. "The doctors say he's perfectly fine."

"And what about . . ." He paused and dropped his voice. "The *box*?"

"Gone," said Kallie, as though slightly surprised at her admission. "I'm officially un-entangled."

"You know, I'm going to research entanglement a bit more. I've talked to my brothers. They said they'd help." He paused and then lit up as though an idea had suddenly popped into his head. "Hey! I heard all about how you saved Anna. Do you think I could write my story about you? You could be my hero!"

Kallie laughed. "I don't think so. I'm not exactly the hero type."

Kallie thought about that word, *hero*, and what it meant. At first, she had thought she was the hero of her story. And in one way, she had saved Anna. Yet, in another important way, she had tried to destroy her. When she had seen the look in Anna's eyes after all the cruel things she had said, it was clear. Kallie had not been the hero at all. In fact, she had been the villain.

Kallie looked around. "Where's Anna?"

They found her sitting at the side of the building, playing a soft tune on her bone flute. The bright light that had always danced in her eyes was now only a faint glimmer.

Kallie wished she could take back her insensitive and callous words. She wanted to tell Anna how wrong she had been, how sorry she was, but as Anna had once told her, people, unlike objects, weren't so easily repaired.

She reached into her satchel and withdrew Anna's clothes. She had washed them, ironed them, and folded them with great care. She handed them to her. "Thank you," Kallie said softly.

Anna nodded.

"Good news—you got enough support with those flyers, and Pole said Mr. Bent got permission from Mr. McEwan, so we can go ahead with planning Periodic Table Day."

Again, Anna nodded.

Kallie grappled for something to say. Something about how wrong she'd been, how cruel and insensitive, but all she could come up with was: "I was thinking, you and I could have a lot of fun dressing up as Kryptonite . . . together."

The glimmer in Anna's eyes flickered, and she smiled. It was a small smile, but a warm one nonetheless. Kallie noticed Pole volleying curious glances between them and then shrugging.

"Come on, Anastasiya," said Kallie. "I've been dying to hear all about your life as a protozoan."

Anna tucked the ocarina along with the clothing into her purple backpack. She held out a hand, and Kallie hauled her to her feet. They headed into the school, the three friends, together.

An atom needs protons, electrons, and neutrons to be complete, thought Kallie.

"You know, class," said Ms. Beausoleil, "it takes a great deal of courage to release the familiar—the seemingly secure—to embrace the new. But I must tell you, there is, in fact, more security in the adventurous and exciting, for in movement there is life, and in change there is power. I'm proud to say someone in this class has taken the first step toward change."

Ms. Beausoleil was right. Kallie was now ready to

accept that there were things out of her control. Or better said, beyond her control. She could still make plans and schedules, choose her clothing and her foods, but some things were part of life's great game of chance.

"Played by quantum physics rules," she whispered to Pole.

"Now," said Ms. Beausoleil, "someone has finished a wonderful story, and I'd like to read it to you. That is, if she'll allow."

All eyes searched the room for the mysterious writer. Was it Queenie? Mathusha? Most faces settled on Anna, who simply shrugged and shook her head.

"Kallie?" said Ms. Beausoleil. There was a collective gasp as all heads turned toward her.

For a moment, Kallie's mind was not in the class. She was on the ferry again with Anna, returning from the festival. She could see the sharp item the faceless man had given her—not a dagger—but a pencil. Anna sat listlessly in a corner, not smiling, not dancing, not even searching for Champ, and Kallie was suddenly sure she knew exactly how to end her story. She knew exactly which character must die.

"Not Kallie," she said to Ms. Beausoleil. "From now on, I'm Kaliope. There is no more Kallie. Kallie is gone."

A knowing smile snaked across Ms. Beausoleil's lips. And for the first time, Kallie thought the woman did sort of sparkle a bit. Like a beautiful sun.

Ms. Beausoleil held the paper in her firm, but kind, hands. Slowly, she began to read.

Long ago, in a land far away, there once lived a bone carver's apprentice who vanquished an evil Empress with the help of the bones of a Lie-peddler . . .

— 35 —

THE LAST BONE

Liah left the palace, the dagger still lying beside the Empress. She could hear the enemy clamoring at the gates, and she knew the Empress's fate was sealed. Someone somewhere beyond her world had made a decision.

Calmly, Liah walked down the mountainside. The wooden boxes were all empty. She had taken all the bones and given them proper burials. Those souls might rest now. Sadly, the bones in the tiny box would never find peace.

She passed the fields of sorghum and millet—no longer soured with evil—now bright gold and ready for harvest. She paused only briefly at the crossroads where she had met the Lie-peddler so long ago, and then entered the ancient forest.

Halfway through it, she stopped. She reached into her

satchel and took out the box. She placed it on the edge of the path, looked up, and smiled.

A figure stood half-hidden in shadow, a white beast at its side. Liah waved.

The figure waved back.

ACKNOWLEDGMENTS

This novel took several years to get right. Without the support of the following people, it may (as Ms. Beausoleil would say) have crumbled like brittle cheese.

A huge thank you goes to my husband, Michael, for reading chapter after chapter, and cheering me on to the finish line. Thank you to my wonderful children for helping out in so many ways and for putting up with my blank stares. Your love and support mean the world to me.

Thank you to my dear friend, Birgit, who sent me a box of Story Cubes some ten years ago. It was the seed that grew into this novel.

It is very difficult to get a setting right when you are not from the area. Though I've visited many times,

I needed local eyes to make sure I had captured not only the physical landscape, but also its mystique. A special thanks goes to author and friend, Jan Gangsei, for lending me her Vermonter eyes and helping me sort out marinas and mountain shadows.

Thank you to the Ontario Arts Council for their support of this work via the Writers' Reserve.

Thank you to illustrator, Yana Bogatch, for her wonderfully evocative and creepy artwork.

Thank you to my superstar agent, John M. Cusick, who waited patiently, offering bushels of encouragement while I sorted this one out.

Thanks to all the staff at Roaring Brook Press who tirelessly support and promote my work. Thank you to copyeditor Kylie Byrd for her eagle eyes.

And last, but never ever least, the biggest thank you goes to my brilliant editor, Emily Feinberg, who thankfully enjoys a creepy story as much as I do and who helped shape and polish this one until it became the best it could be.